# Gwen Iver &
# Pendragon's Puzzle

## Mark Piggott

Curious Corvid
PUBLISHING

To my great nieces and nephews, the future readers that
inspired this story . . .

# A Special Thank You

to the art teachers and students of my alma mater, Phillipsburg High School, in Phillipsburg, N.J., for the chapter art in my story. They are the artists of the next generation I want to support and inspire with my words.

Keith Dwyer

Faith Roncoroni

Kevin Betancur

Jasiah Hardy

Alexa Lau

Emma O'Connor

Ameilia Sirianni

Kaylyn Zahn

Alitheia Kadlub

Ellie Zechman

# Prologue:

## *The Founding*

The waves crashed against the seawall, sheltering the inland cove. The protected shoal swept the coastline from the rocky cliffs to the rich, fertile land above. It was an idyllic place that weathered the storms along this barren section of a great lake—a perfect hideaway for weary travelers seeking a new life.

The air buzzed with a flurry of magical sparks that flowed into a swirling gateway on the rocky shore. An old man stepped through the gate and gazed at his new surroundings. He walked with a rather hefty wooden staff that banged against the rocks with every step. A rather distinguished beard, as white as the driven snow, poured out from beneath his hood. It starkly contrasted against the robe of hewn cloth dyed a vibrant purple that billowed around his lithe form.

He stepped across the slippery rocks and carefully kept his footing as he edged toward the water. Gazing out of the cove, waves broke against the rocks, soaking his feet. "My lady, are you there?" he whispered.

The cove went eerily silent. Waves stopped breaking on the shore, and the water became still like a pane of glass. It began to eddy into a tiny whirlpool before the old man. A golden glow emanated from the center of the swirling vortex. Slowly, a beautiful woman draped in golden chainmail rose from the deep. Her blonde hair shimmered in the dim light as if all the light had drawn in toward her. She stood atop the still waters, leaning on a gleaming long sword with a magnificent, jeweled hilt.

The old man bowed, recognizing her authority. "My dear Lady of the Lake, it has been too long," he said with a smile, joyous at seeing her.

"It warms my heart to see you, too, Merlin, my old friend. I assume your search has been fruitful."

"It has. This will be a perfect spot to build our community," he replied, motioning to their surroundings. "It is hidden, far from the reaches of the mortal world, even at their current rate of expansion and exploration. It will be centuries before they reach us here. That will give us time to establish and unite as a community."

"And the others? Are they in agreement with our plan?"

Merlin sighed heavily, gathering his thoughts before addressing the delicate situation. "Reluctantly, but yes," he began. "There are still many old grievances and hatreds to be resolved, but that will ease with time. They all understand that this is the only way to ensure our survival in this modern age."

"And Guinevere, can she travel?"

"She is heavy with a child but ready and able to protect the Pendragon."

"I am happy to hear that, but it is a heavy burden to be laid upon the queen and her descendants. They will need supervision and guidance along the way."

"I will bear that responsibility, my Lady. I will build my tower up there," Merlin said, pointing to the cliff above the entrance to the cove. "That will allow me to watch over our new home."

"Then I will join you, my friend," the Lady of the Lake replied. Holding the magnificent sword, she walked across the water and stepped onto the rocks with Merlin. "I could not let you carry this burden on your own. We will do this together to protect the Pendragon and the magic."

"Are you sure about this, my Lady? Without your presence, the waters may grow turbulent and uneasy."

"I will make my home here, by the water's edge, to ensure that doesn't happen," she assured him.

"And what of *Excalibur*? Should we give it to the queen?"

They both stared at the sword she held. The blade shined, with a sharp and clean edge. Its golden hilt glimmered even in the dim light of the cove.

"*Excalibur* is the king's sword. It is a symbol of the power of the Pendragon. Symbols need to be seen to be appreciated." The Lady of the Lake spun about and heaved the sword. It sailed over the water toward a towering rock at the cove's entrance. It was a tall, slender rock caressed by the water with every wave that struck against it. The sword landed on the top of the stone monolith, embedded up to the hilt. The sword and the stone were united again. The Lady of the Lake smiled when the deed was done.

"Now, let us summon our Fae kin and bring them to their new home."

## Chapter One:

### *First Day of School*

Gwen Iver rushed around her room, desperate to find something appropriate to wear for the first day of high school in Camelot Cove. Her clothes were strewn about her bed, dresser, and closet. Her blonde hair was brushed, her makeup done, and all she needed now was the right outfit. She wanted to make a good impression. She remembered what her friend Triss often said . . . *"Always dress like it's the best day of your life!"*

Gwen Iver was an eclectic girl. Her room resembled any teenage girl's bedroom, with posters of movie stars and boy bands hanging on the walls. Her desk faced out of her second-story window, looking across the lake. It was a view that inspired her every morning. Sitting beside an old-fashioned record player, she had a small crate filled with vinyl LPs. Whenever she listened to the music, it reminded her of a bygone era.

She tried so many different outfit variations that it made her head spin. She didn't know which one to wear. "Gwen! Get down here and eat your breakfast or you're going to be late!" a gruff voice shouted from the kitchen below. It seemed to rattle every door and window in the house with its mighty bellow.

"Okay, Uncle Merle, I'm coming!" she replied before giving up on trying to style herself. She finally decided to be herself in a simple skirt and blouse—demure yet classy. Gwen rushed down the stairs, taking a moment to blow kisses on the portraits of her mom and dad hanging on the wall. It was something she did every morning to remember her parents.

They were very young in these pictures, barely out of their teens. She remembered so little of her parents except for the love she still carried from them in her heart. A boating accident left Gwen an orphan in the care of her guardian, her uncle, Merle Iver. He was her only real family in this sleepy coastal town situated on the shores of Lake Superior in the Northern Peninsula of Michigan.

Gwen hurried into the kitchen, where Merle stood over the stove, cooking bacon and eggs for breakfast. The smell intoxicated the teenager as she sat down to eat, but on her plate was an ominous presence. A wooden puzzle box sat there as if daring her to try and open it.

"Oh, come on, Uncle Merle, do I have to do this today? It's my first day of high school!"

"Just because you're starting school doesn't mean you stop training your mind," he said as he continued to cook. "Now come on, yearling. Get to it while I finish your eggs." He flipped over an egg timer on the stove as her countdown began.

Gwen scowled as she picked up the puzzle box. She had just turned fifteen and felt more alive than ever, but her Uncle Merle treated her like a porcelain doll. She hated it when he called her "yearling"—a term of endearment to him but a reminder to Gwen that he still thought of her as a child. As much as she loved her guardian, she could not wait for the day when she could leave him and his overbearing demands behind.

Gwen shifted the pieces around the wooden box, similar to a Rubik's Cube, and tried to put them in the correct order to open the box. There were letters carved in some of the pieces, like old Viking runes, but she never understood them or what they meant. The puzzle was quite challenging, and no matter how hard she tried, Gwen couldn't open it. It frustrated the teenager to no end. Uncle Merle had been torturing her with this box for several years with no hint of how to solve the puzzle. "With patience comes understanding!" was the only advice he ever gave about the box, telling her that the prize inside was worth the effort.

Merle finished cooking the eggs as the last grain of sand dropped through the egg timer. "Time's up," he announced, turning to the table and depositing the eggs on her plate before taking the puzzle box away. Gwen pursed her lips and huffed at her uncle, crossing her arms in frustration and disgust. Merle put the puzzle box back on the shelf over the stove before putting plates of bacon and toast on the table.

"Stop your whining. You'll get it eventually." Merle gently patted her head. "Now, eat your breakfast." Reluctantly, Gwen picked up her fork and started eating her eggs. After the first bite, her hunger overwhelmed her, and she grabbed some bacon and a piece of toast as she devoured her food.

"Slow down, yearling. You'll give yourself an upset stomach," Merle said as he poured her a glass of orange juice. Gwen listened to her guardian and began to pace herself. "So, are you ready for your first day?"

Gwen finished chewing the food in her mouth and swallowed before answering. "As ready as I'm going to be," she said, drinking some juice to wash down her breakfast.

"I'm worried about Morgan and her Dreadmoor gang. They seem to run the school, but Lance and Artie told me not to worry about them."

"Well, just stay away from Morgan Moor. She's nothing but trouble," Merle advised as he sat down to eat his breakfast, wagging his spatula at Gwen. "And I don't like that kid brother of hers either. That boy never stands up to her, or for himself for that matter."

"First off, Uncle Merle, Artie is her stepbrother," Gwen explained. "Secondly, he's been one of my best friends since middle school. Lance says he's just not all that confident in himself. Maybe high school will turn things around for him."

Merle huffed as they continued eating. The two quietly finished their breakfast as neither wanted to belabor the argument that the other would not concede. It was a strange yet solid part of their relationship. Gwen looked at the time and panicked before she shoved the last piece of toast in her mouth and grabbed her book bag.

"Shoot, I'm late!" she mumbled. "I promised Viv I'd stop by on my way to school!"

"Say hi to my lady for me," Merle said as he scarfed down his food.

"Why do you do that, Uncle Merle? Call Viv 'my lady' all the time? Was there ever something between you two?"

"It is a term of respect and endearment, something your generation needs to learn," Merle explained, wagging his fork at her. "Viviane is the reason Camelot Cove has prospered over the years. I respect her hard work to preserve our way of life. Now, run along, or you'll be late."

Gwen didn't say another word, although she had more questions. With a quick wave, she ran out the door and headed to school. For Gwen, it was a bit longer of a trek than most of the kids in town. She and her Uncle Merle lived at the lighthouse atop the rocky cliff overlooking the entrance to the cove. The tiny house was comfortable enough for the two of them, but it made life difficult for the teenager. She hopped on her bike and raced down the road, following the rock-strewn edge from Lookout Point along the coastline until she hit the town of Camelot Cove.

It was a quiet, sleepy little town on the shores of Lake Superior on the Upper Peninsula of Michigan. The community was said to have been founded by European settlers exploring the new world, but precisely who founded the town was a long-running debate. The only clue to its origin was the rusted sword embedded in the rock at the entrance to the cove. Some say it was a Viking sword, while others thought it was English, Dutch, or French. Either way, that symbol was where they got the name Camelot Cove.

The town was best known for its fishing. The deep waters outside the cove were some of the best fishing grounds for walleye, northern pike, smallmouth bass, and perch. Anglers worldwide flocked to Camelot Cove to take advantage of these prime fisheries, so the community relied on them year-round for economic survival and stability. From the hotels and restaurants along the boardwalk to the tackle shops, fishing boats, and ferry service at the pier, the entire town benefitted from this way of life.

As Gwen rode down the hill and into the harbor, people waved hello and shouted greetings to her. Being a small town, everyone knew everybody, so they all got along for the most part. After her parents' deaths, the community helped Merle raise the orphan girl.

"Good morning, Gwen!" shouted Gerald Duffy as he carried a tower of boxes holding fruits and vegetables to place for sale out front of Sherwood's General Store. Gwen waved as she watched him effortlessly haul fresh produce from the local farms. She was always amazed how someone so skinny could easily carry such heavy boxes around.

"Mornin', Gwen, dear!" greeted Edna McMullen as she opened her flower shop, The Secret Garden. Even for someone rumored to be nearly eighty, she still had a spring in her step, although she would never admit her actual age. Still, Gwen admired how delicate she was with plants and flowers, always mindful of their natural beauty.

She pedaled across the Broadmoor Boardwalk, past the King's Arms Hotel, the Witches Brew Coffee Shop, the Vikings Table restaurant, and other eateries, shops, and storefronts that kept the guests who came to Camelot Cove entertained, well-fed, and loaded down with souvenirs.

Finally, she reached the pier. As she approached the dockside area, she saw a familiar face waiting for her.

Artie Moor sat on his bike and leaned against a stack of crawfish traps nestled at the head of the pier. His torn jeans and comic book t-shirt demonstrated his casual style and no-nonsense attitude toward the world around him. His light brown hair fell around his head as he ran his fingers through it like a comb. A boyish appearance was hidden behind wire-rimmed glasses that looked like they had been repeatedly repaired. When he spotted Gwen riding down the docks, he smiled and waved to her as relief washed over him.

"About time!" he shouted. "We're gonna be late!"

"Sorry, but it took me forever to pick out what I would wear," she answered before stopping beside him. He looked up and down at her clothes before laughing.

"It took you all morning to pick out that?"

Gwen punched him in the arm for his snide remark. "You're one to talk," she said before pushing off from a standstill, pedaling past Artie, and heading toward the pier.

"Where are you going? We're going to be late as it is!"

"I've got to see Viv quick," she said as she rode on. "It won't take long." Artie shook his head in disbelief and looked nervously at his watch before he spun his bike around and chased after her. The two rode down to the end of the pier to a dingy old shack. The sign read *Lake Lady Boat Rentals* in big bold letters. The boat shop was opening for business as the shutters were swung out and locked in place by an old woman dressed in yellow rain gear and heavy rubber boots. Her long gray hair was pulled back into a ponytail, flopping outside her raincoat. She smoked a pipe, held firm between her teeth as smoke circled her head.

"Morning, Viv!" Gwen shouted. Viv turned and saw the two kids riding hard and fast down the pier.

"Hiya Gwen, Arthur—" she started to say before she pulled out a pocket watch from inside her coat and looked at the time. "You're running a little behind, kiddo. You better skedaddle off to school."

"I know, I know, I just wanted to stop by and get my last summer paycheck," Gwen said. "I need the money for school supplies."

"What's the matter? Merle being a tightwad again?" Viv asked before she stepped inside her shack.

"No, he got me some basic supplies, but a lighthouse keeper doesn't pay enough for an old man and a teenage girl. I like to help out when I can." Viv stepped outside and handed Gwen a wad of cash, her last paycheck for working at the boat shack over the summer months. Gwen quickly tucked the money away in her pocket.

"You got a heart of gold, Gwen Iver. Never forget that. Now, get going, you two. You might make the first bell if you try," Viv said, shooing the two away.

"Fat chance of that. See you, Ms. Viv!" Artie joked as he took off ahead of Gwen.

"Bye, Viv! See you after school!" Gwen shouted with a wave. Viv waved back as they raced toward Camelot Cove High School. She was curious why Viv pulled her watch out of her pocket again. She seemed to be adjusting the time as a tiny bell chimed abruptly before Viv closed the lid and tucked it away. Gwen wondered about that wicked smirk on Viv's face as she went about her business at the pier.

# Chapter Two:

## *The Dreadmoor Gang*

Gwen and Artie pedaled as fast as possible, praying they would make it to the school grounds before the first bell. Neither of them bothered to look at their watches for fear of losing precious time they didn't have. However, as they approached the school, they were surprised to see people still milling about outside. Gwen looked at her watch and saw they had five minutes to spare.

"What? How is that—" she started to say until a familiar voice interrupted.

"Hey, freshmen, about time you got here!" Lance du Lok shouted. The sophomore strolled up to his two friends and flashed a smile. His dashing good looks, wavy black hair, and crisp, smart dress made him the B.M.O.C. or "Big Man on Campus" at Camelot Cove High School. He had everything going for him in school—a star athlete, top scholar, community volunteer, and student council leader. Above all else, Lance was loyal to a fault. His loyalty went above and beyond his family and friends.

"We thought we were going to be late, Lance. It looks like we made it just in time," Artie said as he and Gwen hopped off their bikes and walked over to the bike rack to chain them up.

"Just barely, freshman. You two better head over to the auditorium for your orientation."

"And which one is the auditorium?" Gwen asked.

Lance shook his head in disbelief. "Didn't you tour the campus over the summer?" he asked. Gwen and Artie shrugged their shoulders.

"Sorry, but my family doesn't own most of the luxury waterfront property in Camelot Cove," Artie snapped back. "Some of us need to work over the summer to make spending money."

"Knock it off, Artie. Lance is only trying to help," Gwen scolded. "Besides, we had plenty of time to do the tour but decided to go swimming off Nimue Point, remember?" Artie couldn't argue with her logic and gave in.

"Come on. I'll show you where to go before I head off to homeroom." Lance led as the two freshmen followed him across campus. Camelot Cove High School—Home of the Dragons—was a small school with less than 300 students in the entire school. However, the school has a long heritage with top marks in education and athletics. They also had a penchant for their share of bullies and troublemakers.

"Well, well, well . . . Look what the cat dragged in," snarked Maude Reddy, who was loitering by the main entrance with other members of the Dreadmoor Gang. Maude, a bit of a tomboy, expressed her personality through purple-dyed hair pulled back to expose the shaved sides of her head and the multiple piercings on her ears, nose, and eyebrows. She twirled a toothpick around her mouth like a cigarette, chewing it repeatedly. The rest of the Dreadmoor Gang were an odd mixture of students, but they all wore the same leather vest with a logo on the back—a single eye with a lightning bolt through it.

"Give it a rest, Maude. We're already late as it is," Artie said. Maude sneered and looked at him as if she considered him a waste of space.

"Shut your yap, momma's boy. I wasn't talking to you," she said, pushing Artie aside and walking up to Gwen. Although Maude stood a head taller, Gwen never backed down. "Just remember this, princess. You don't have your old lighthouse keeper to protect you now. You're on our turf. The Dreadmoor Gang runs this school, so you do what we say, got it?"

"I don't listen to you or anyone in Morgan Moor's gang, Maude," Gwen said defiantly, pushing her way past Maude. Maude moved to hit Gwen, but Lance grabbed her hand to stop her.

"I wouldn't do anything to get suspended on the first day of school, Maude," he said, keeping a firm grip on her wrist. "Besides, as a freshman, you don't want to be late for orientation either." No matter how hard she struggled, Maude couldn't break free. A loud whistle broke their concentration as Maude and Lance turned to see Morgan Moor standing across the way. Her beauty was undeniable to anyone who saw her—long black hair, perfectly manicured nails, deep red lips, standing tall on high heels in a miniskirt and silk shirt. She was the uncrowned queen of Camelot High School, and her Dreadmoor Gang enforced her reign.

Lance let go of Maude's wrist as he followed Artie and Gwen into school. Maude sneered and spat on the ground, cursing at Gwen under her breath. She barely noticed it as Morgan casually approached her gang of juvenile delinquents. "What did you stop me for, Morgan? We need to teach those newbies exactly who is in charge, especially the little priss, Gwen Iver."

Morgan said nothing to her protege but instead slapped her across the face. Maude rubbed her cheek, feeling the sting from her slap. "What did I tell you, Maude? Gwen Iver is off-limits until I say so. She is an empty vessel right now. Once she possesses the power of the Pendragon, you can do whatever you want to get her to relinquish it to me." Morgan suddenly grabbed Maude by the face, squeezing her cheeks and jaw tightly between her fingers. "But until then, you leave her alone, got it?"

Maude vigorously shook her head, desperate for Morgan to let her go. Morgan looked around at the other members of the Dreadmoor Gang until all nodded in agreement. Finally, Morgan let Maude go and strolled into school. "Get a move on, or you'll be late," she reminded them. The gang shrugged off the inevitable and slowly followed her into school.

Maude hung back, coming in last, as she rubbed the pain away in her jaw and cheeks. She hated it when Morgan singled her out, but Maude knew who was in charge and always fell in line. For now, she would do what Morgan said, but when the time came, Maude would take out all her aggression on Gwen Iver over and over again.

Day one of high school was more pomp and circumstance, lectures, and introductions instead of actual teaching. Gwen and Artie spent most of the day bored out of their minds, only getting slightly reprieved at lunch, where they enjoyed their day with their friends. After the school day ended, Gwen and Artie watched football practice from the bleachers. Lance did his part on the field as the quarterback, leading his team through offensive drills.

Artie visibly scowled as he watched the practice from the stands. He envied Lance, and it showed. Gwen didn't understand the reasons behind his constant jealousy. The three of them had been friends since middle school. Lance excelled academically and in sports more than Gwen and Artie, but she attributed that to his upper-class upbringing. The du Lok family owned many profitable waterfront properties and employed most of the townsfolk, making them the wealthiest family in Camelot Cove. Even still, Lance never let his family or their money get in the way of his friendship with them.

"Come on, Artie, why do you have to hold a grudge over Lance just because he's from a wealthy family?" Gwen argued. "Lance doesn't act like the rest of the du Loks, and you know it."

"I'm not holding a grudge. I just—" Artie paused for a moment before he answered. "I just hate how 'Mister Perfect' is good at everything he does while I can barely keep my grades above average. I mean, how am I supposed to compete with that for your . . ." Artie abruptly stopped his rant. Gwen, however, heard his little confession and was curious to hear what else he had to say.

"Compete for my what?" Gwen asked slyly. She had known how Artie felt about her for a long time, but he was too shy to admit it. He sat there on the bleacher, blushing bright red while squirming in his seat, trying desperately not to look over at Gwen.

Gwen knew Artie and Lance had feelings for her and felt the same about them, but she kept it on the level of a mutual friendship. She did not want to choose one and hurt the other, so Gwen kept them close but distant for now. She decided to let nature take its course to see where love would take her.

"Ah, is Arthur finally confessing his true feelings?" asked Triss Paul as she and her brother, G Wayne Paul, walked up the bleachers to join Gwen and Artie. The Black siblings were stellar opposites in style and appearance. Triss was a sophomore, statuesque and trendy, with a perfectly tressed afro, blinged sunglasses, and wearing the latest fashion as if she just stepped out of a magazine. Her brother, Gregory, a freshman who preferred to be called by his online gamer handle, G Wayne, stared at his cell phone as he tapped away mindlessly. He wore thick-rimmed glasses, a simple shirt buttoned to the top, untucked over his jeans. He looked dressed down compared to his sister.

"Oh, give me a break, Triss," Artie snapped as he scooted over and made room for Triss to sit next to Gwen, and because he wanted to avoid further embarrassment, turned his back to the girls and focused on talking to G Wayne.

"Don't tease him, Triss," Gwen whispered to her friend. "It's hard for Artie to express his feelings. I mean, look at his family, especially Morgan."

"Oh honey, don't get me started on Morgan Moor. It's only the first day of school, and the queen has begun her reign," Triss complained. "That girl struts around the school like a divine goddess, as if we are her stepping stone to world domination."

"I wouldn't put it past her," Gwen joked. "Since Morgan formed that sleazy little gang of hers, she's been slowly gaining ground around Camelot Cove. Not just the school but shops on the boardwalk and around the harbor. She's got her greedy little paws into a little bit of everything."

"She hates it when someone has something she wants," Artie interjected. "If anyone says no to her, she'll just use the Dreadmoor Gang to 'change' their minds for them." Artie threw up some air quotes emphasizing how ruthless the Dreadmoor Gang could be.

"I heard they got Billy Baker to pay up for protection after his bike shop was vandalized," G Wayne recalled. "And the police won't touch them."

"Of course not. Why would dear old dad push back against his precious little daughter?" Artie lamented. "Why do you think I have it so rough, being the stepson of Sheriff Ulysses Moor?"

Everyone could hear the pain in Artie's voice when he talked about his broken family. After his mother died, his stepfather brushed him aside, focusing all his attention on Morgan, his flesh and blood. Artie spends more time at the local library buried in his books rather than at home. Books were a refuge from the hard life he endured. Gwen wanted to help Artie through these next four years so he could leave the Moor family behind and start a new life.

"Well, cheer up, Artie. With Gwen and me watching your back, you have nothing to fear from your wicked stepsister," Triss stated with a simple pat on his head. Gwen knew she meant well, and Artie seemed to appreciate the sentiment.

"Gee, Triss, does this mean we're going steady?" Artie joked.

"No offense, sugar, but you're not my type," Triss smiled.

"What, too young?"

"Too male!" she said gleefully with a wayward glance. "Don't worry, Artie. There's hope for you yet." Her comment gave Gwen a good laugh, as she never considered herself anyone's type.

"Hey, what about me?" G Wayne argued with his sister.

"You've always got your damn nose buried in your computer or video games, G Wayne," Triss snapped. "You're about as useless as a screen door on a submarine." Everyone laughed, including G Wayne. Gwen knew he could not fault his sister when she was right.

# Chapter Three:

## *Unlocking the Puzzle Box*

After football practice, Lance and Artie escorted Gwen home as usual. It was a casual bike ride through town, with a necessary stop to grab a snack from Rosina's Sweet Shop. After sipping a warm mocha latte from the Witches Brew coffee shop, they made one final stop for school supplies from Grimm's Inkwell stationery store. With a wave to Viv as they rode past the harbor, the trio took the road along the coast to the lighthouse. They eventually hopped off and walked their bikes up the steep hill toward the end of the ride. Walking to the lighthouse gave the friends a chance to talk.

"The team looks terrific out there, Lance. You have a good chance at beating Chelsea this year," Gwen said.

"Yeah, I'd like to win a state championship at least once before I graduate," Lance remarked.

"With that front line protecting you, you can do anything on the field. Those guys live up to their nickname of the football team's 'Monster Squad,'" Artie replied.

"Yeah, but if I don't do my job as quarterback, all their efforts will be in vain," Lance said. "It'll be a good test to get our act together this season."

"I still don't know how you remember your way around the school," Gwen interjected. "That place is a maze."

"You'll get used to it once you get into a routine of where your classes are. It's good that you and Artie are in many of the same classes. That should make it easier for both of you."

"Yeah, but that little witch Maude is in some of them too. It makes my skin crawl having her breathing down my neck," Gwen said. "I don't understand what beef she has with me."

"I wish I could tell you. All I know is that Morgan keeps her on a tight leash. If she didn't, Maude Reddy would explode like the loose cannon she is," Artie concluded. With that, the three finally reached Gwen's house and the lighthouse. The sun was beginning to set as the lighthouse beacon started spinning, casting its glow across the water.

"Uncle Merle must be up in the lighthouse. Good, it gives me a chance to get your help."

"Help with what?" Lance asked. They parked their bikes, and Gwen led them inside to the kitchen. She quickly pulled the puzzle box from the shelf above the stove and showed it to Lance and Artie.

"Is Merle still trying to get you to figure out this thing? It's been what, five years since he started doing that?" Artie asked.

"Yeah, and he said I have to figure it out on my own, but since he's not here, I thought I'd show it to the both of you and get your opinion."

Lance looked over the box first, shifting a few blocks to see how it worked, before handing it over to Artie. "It reminds me of one of those old puzzle cubes from the '80s, but I don't see a specific way to open it," Lance observed. Artie looked at the four corners, examining every aspect, especially the engraved Viking runes.

"How have you been moving the pieces on the box? Right to left, or left to right?" Artie asked.

Gwen thought about it before answering. "Left to right, I guess, but what does it matter?"

"Well, these Viking runes are the key. You read runes based on a three-stone draw. First, you interpret the rune on the right as representing your current situation. Then, look to the rune in the center to represent your challenge. After that, read the rune on the left as an action you can take to address your challenge."

"Okay, wait a minute, how do you know so much about Viking runes?" Lance asked.

"I've been studying Viking runes. I'm going to climb Founder's Rock and look at that sword. I want to know if it is a Viking sword," Artie replied.

"Are you kidding? No one's ever climbed Founder's Rock," Lance teased his young friend.

"Hey, you have your goals, and I have mine!" Artie shot back before Gwen intervened to prevent an impending altercation.

"Can we focus on the box before Uncle Merle gets back? So, what do the runes mean, Artie?"

Artie spun the box in his hand to show what he meant. "This one is the only rune on the right. This is *Eihwaz*, meaning your ability to achieve your goal with resilience. That's your current situation." He turned it again to another rune on the center of the side. "This is *Kaunaz*, your challenge, and it means power." He turned it to the only rune on the left of the box. "The last one is *Dagaz*, how to address your challenge."

"And what does that one mean?" Gwen asked.

"It means awakening. That's what you've been doing wrong. You've been trying to open it backward. You must go right to left, not left to right."

Artie returned the puzzle box to Gwen as she looked at it again, but this time in a new light. Carefully examining the puzzle, she asked Lance to start the egg timer on the stove.

"What? Why?" Lance asked with a laugh.

"If I do this, I'm going to do it as I have always done," she said with determination. Lance reached over and flipped the egg-timer hourglass. Immediately, Gwen went to work, shifting the blocks right to left, working through the puzzle with a newfound desire and will to finally beat the challenge. She worked fervently, clicking the blocks one after another. The grains of sand slowly fell through until Gwen clicked the last block in place as the final grain dropped. There was an audible "click" as the lid popped up, and she knew she had done it. The box was open.

After all the years of trying, Gwen couldn't believe she had finally opened the box. She knew Uncle Merle would be angry that she did it without him here and with Lance and

Artie's help, but none of that mattered. This problem that had plagued her life was finally put to rest.

Carefully, she lifted the lid, her hand shaking in anticipation of seeing what was inside. However, her excitement turned to dismay to see an empty box when she lifted it. There was nothing inside it at all. "Are you freakin' kidding me?" she screamed. "It's empty?"

"Really?" Artie said as he and Lance leaned over Gwen's shoulder to look inside the empty puzzle box. "But I thought your uncle said a prize was inside it?"

"Yeah, well, as usual, Uncle Merle 'stretched' the truth!" Gwen shook the box and noticed a faint glow emanating from inside. She wondered if it was a reflection or something else. Gwen reached inside to feel around the edges, except her hand never touched anything. She kept feeling around for something solid, but her fingers grasped air.

"There's got to be something in here." Suddenly, her arm was forcefully pulled into the box from her fingertips up to her bicep. "What the hell? It's sucking in my arm!" she screamed, panicking. She tried but could not pull her arm out.

"Get it off me! Get it off me!" Lance and Artie grabbed Gwen and the box, desperately trying to separate the two, but the box would not let go, no matter how hard they pulled. "Ow, it burns!" she cried as tears started streaming down her face from the pain. "Help me! Help me, please!"

"What are you three doing?" Merle shouted when he walked into the kitchen. Once he saw the box on Gwen's arm, Merle looked at his charge dumbfounded. "Damn it all, Gwen, you weren't supposed to open it without me here. What in the world were you thinking?"

"Can you scold me later, Uncle Merle? Just get this thing off me! It hurts bad!"

"I know it does, yearling, but you no longer have a choice. It would be best if you let it finish what it started. Let Gwen go, boys." Lance and Artie were visibly confused, but with one look at Merle, they did as they were told and backed away. They relented and did as they were told and backed away from her. Gwen couldn't believe what was happening.

She clawed at the box with her free hand, desperate to get free, and Merle just stood there and watched. *Why isn't he helping me?*

"Don't worry, Gwen. We're here with you. Let the magic do the work, yearling. Don't fight it, and you'll be fine."

Gwen was scared out of her wits, but her uncle's comforting words struck a chord deep inside her. She took a deep breath and gave in to whatever the box was doing to her. The pain subsided as soon as she stopped struggling to free herself. The pain turned from a burning sensation to warmth like the sun on a summer beach.

Within moments, the box slid effortlessly off her arm and to the floor. To everyone's surprise, a golden armor now encased Gwen's arm. It resembled medieval plate armor forged over chain mail, extending from her right hand to her shoulder. It looked heavy, but to Gwen, it was as if it was not even there. She could barely feel the weight of it at all, nor did it encumber her movements. Lance and Artie looked in awe, shocked by how it all happened. Uncle Merle, on the other hand, was not fazed at all.

He bent down and picked up the box, returning it to its place on the shelf over the stove. "Well, you certainly caused a kerfuffle, didn't you?" Merle said, astonishing Gwen but also getting on her last nerve.

"Me? What the heck is going on, Uncle Merle? What is this thing, and why can't I take it off?"

Merle did not answer her, nor did he turn around to look at her. Instead, he slammed his fists into the counter, startling Gwen and the others. In all their years together, Gwen had never seen Merle get physical, not with her or anyone. He always seemed to be able to talk his way out of any bad situation, all the more reason that this fit of anger scared her.

"There are rules, Gwen Iver, rules I set specifically for your protection, and you broke them," he shouted before turning around to glare at her. "But it's too late now. The deed is done. It's time for you to learn everything. Come with me . . . all of you."

Merle stormed out the door toward the lighthouse, and Gwen and the others quickly followed. Once inside, Merle secured the door with several heavy-duty locks. Gwen was no stranger to all the security, but she figured it was Merle's way of trying to keep people out and from damaging the lighthouse. There was, however, another reason for them.

When he latched the final lock, Merle moved to the center of the structure. "Come on, you three, get over here," he ordered. The three teenagers did as they were told and gathered in the center of the lighthouse. Merle walked over to the broom closet and yanked out a crooked old staff hidden behind a dust broom and a mop.

With each step, he transformed from an old lighthouse keeper into a sorcerer in flowing robes. Moving toward Gwen, Lance, and Artie, he seemingly glided across the floor. His overalls and plaid shirt magically wove into a hooded purple and gold robe. Even his beard and hair grew out in length during the transformation.

Uncle Merle was gone. All that was left was what appeared to be something out of one of Gwen's fantasy video games. He tapped his staff on different stones on the floor. Each stone he touched glowed with a rune. When he finished, the floor around the outer edge of the lighthouse dropped to form a staircase that disappeared into the darkness below.

Merle tapped his staff one last time, and the tip glowed a light blue, as bright as a lantern, to illuminate the way. The old man said nothing as he walked over and descended into the cavern below. Gwen was frightened but intrigued as she bravely took the first steps, following him down the stairs as Lance and Artie followed close behind.

The stone staircase spiraled down. As the three friends walked, the steps became damp with moisture. The echoing sound of waves crashing against the rocks could be heard.

"Do you hear that?" Artie asked his friends. "This must be one of those sea caves near the entrance to the cove."

"I thought those caves were inaccessible due to the constant pounding of the surf?" Lance said.

Gwen had yet to respond. She flexed her golden arm as so many questions swirled through her brain about the armor, the man she called uncle, and everything that had happened to her. She needed answers to these questions as they slowly descended into the cavern below.

They stopped on a ledge overlooking a sea cave. Water bubbled up and splashed through the small openings in the rock wall from Lake Superior. A constant dripping sound could be heard from the collection of moisture on the stalactites jutting downward from the ceiling above into the water below. The light from the staff reflected off the water and the tiny droplets clinging to the rocks around them. It was like a mirror ball, sending thousands of dancing lights around the room.

"What is this place?" Gwen asked.

"It is my inner sanctum and the heart of the Pendragon!" Merle exclaimed, his voice relayed in a booming echo off the cavern walls.

"The Pendragon? What do you mean? What's going on, Uncle Merle?" Gwen asked, frustrated and confused.

"My name is not Merle Iver. I use that name to live and interact with the people of the outside world," he said, turning around to face her, Lance, and Artie. "My true name is one you may have heard from long ago . . . Merlin. I am the sorcerer responsible for protecting the Pendragon, our world's ancient source of magic. This cave is where that power resides."

The three teenagers were stunned by his admission, but the ground rumbled before they could ask questions. Something within the cavern was moving. It was enormous and powerful, breaking through the water below. Rising slowly behind Merlin was a massive golden dragon with scales resembling the armor now encasing Gwen's right arm. Its eyes glowed with the same magical light that emanated from Merlin's staff. The massive creature filled the cave.

"Please tell me I'm not the only one that sees a dragon," Artie softly whispered as Lance and Gwen nodded in agreement.

Gwen could see that the boys were terrified, afraid to move an inch, but not her. Gwen's eyes were filled with awe as if the dragon was something from a dream. She walked toward the edge of the precipice, moving closer to the creature. Lance and Artie reached out to stop her, but Merlin lowered his staff to prevent them from interfering.

Gwen held out her armored hand. The dragon leaned down and let her caress its nose, petting it like a dog or a cat. Gwen showed no fear of the majestic creature as she felt a strange connection between them. The dragon backed away, bowed to Gwen, and descended into the water below. Within seconds, it disappeared.

The cave went silent as Gwen blinked her eyes as if waking from a trance. "For more than two thousand years, I have protected the heirs of Pendragon," Merlin explained as he approached Gwen. "The line has been passed from generation to generation and now resides in you, Gwen Iver. Your mother should have brought you down here to explain things to you, but her murder turned that task over to me."

"Murder? I thought Mom and Dad died in a boating accident," Gwen said.

"They did, but that accident was caused by an outside force, from someone trying to steal the Pendragon. Some people would corrupt the magic for their own twisted purposes. I tried to stop them, but it was too late. Once your mother died, the power of the Pendragon returned to the box, where it has laid dormant, waiting for you to open it and receive the gift from within."

Merlin dragged the tip of his staff across her arm. The armor reacted to the magic, sparkling like fireflies dancing across a summer meadow. "The Pendragon protects you as you defend it, ensuring that the magic flows freely, unimpeded and untainted. That is your destiny, Gwen Iver. You are descended from those who swore an oath to the Pendragon."

"Descended from who?" Gwen asked.

"Long ago, after the death of good King Arthur, the Lady of the Lake and I came to this place we now call Camelot Cove," Merlin explained. "We needed a place, somewhere secluded, where the Pendragon and those gifted with its magic could thrive and live in peace. The Fae leaders forged a pact—to live together in peace, protected by this ancient magic. Your ancestor was the first to wield such power. . . Queen Guinevere.

The name struck a chord with Gwen—Guinevere, Queen of Camelot, consort of King Arthur. Somehow, Gwen was related to these royal figures from the legends of ancient Britain, Camelot, the Knights of the Round Table, and so much more.

"Are you saying I'm descended from royalty? I mean, related to King Arthur?" Gwen asked.

"Indeed, you are yearling. You are a Princess of Avalon, the rightful heir. Since the death of King Arthur, the power of the Pendragon has been handed down to the women in your family and carried on through generations. The Fae—those born of magic—have lived here for over two thousand years."

"Fae? Born of magic? What do you mean?" Artie inquired.

"We call them Fae, but generally, the term is used to describe anyone born of or touched by magic: fairies, elves, dwarves, ogres, centaurs, goblins, merfolk, witches, warlocks, and others. They live here in Camelot Cove, along with their human allies. We came together so that these magical beings would no longer be hunted and scorned by humans.”

“But there's nothing like that in Camelot Cove,” Lance argued. “Everyone here is human.”

“Merlin!” a voice shouted, interrupting the discussion. They looked up to see Viv rapidly descending the stairs. “What the devil is going on here?” Before anyone could answer, Viv spotted the golden armor on Gwen's arm. “How on earth did that happen?”

“I'm sorry, my lady, but she broke the rules and opened the box without me. There was nothing I could do,” Merlin explained. Viv walked over to Gwen, taking her by the arm as she ran her hand across the armor. It sparked to life, igniting some magical fireworks into the air.

“Viv, you too? You knew about all of this?” Gwen argued.

“Well, of course, I did. Merlin and I have been looking after you, preparing you for this moment,” she explained, caressing Gwen's face with her other hand while examining her armored form. “The armor is incomplete. You haven't fully accepted the power of the Pendragon.”

"Accept it? Why should I? All the people I've known and loved did nothing but lie to my face about who I am and what happened to my parents! I never asked for this! I never wanted this, and now you expect me to give up all my hopes and dreams because of some misbegotten family lineage?" Gwen stormed out of the cave and ran up the stairs, tears streaming down her face. She was so overwhelmed with emotion that all she could do was run away.

Viv sighed, worried about how this frightened girl would accept the responsibilities laid upon her tender shoulders. "Go after her, lads," Viv told Lance and Artie. "It's up to you to look after Gwen and protect her from harm."

"Harm? Who would want to hurt her?" Artie asked.

"The same ones that killed her parents," Merlin said. "With the power of the Pendragon incomplete, there is a chance they could capture her and force her to relinquish it. You must not let anything happen to her until she fully accepts the gift and the responsibility that comes with it."

Viv knew the boys would protect Gwen as Lance and Artie chased after her. Viv remained with Merlin, calculating a solution to the predicament. "I am so sorry, my lady. I did not anticipate her attempting to open the box alone as she did. Otherwise, I would have told her sooner. I fear we may have lost her trust."

"I know, but her heart is pure and sound. It will take time, but Gwen will accept the power of the Pendragon. I do not doubt that."

"But what if she discovers the truth about her parents' deaths?" Merlin inquired. "If she uncovers that Morgan Moor was responsible for their murders, it might push her over the edge. And then, we'll lose her forever."

"Or it may lead her to the truth about who she truly is," Viv responded, but another thought came to mind. "What if I showed her who the Fae are by granting her the fairy sight?"

"My lady, is that wise? I don't know if she can handle such a revelation."

"We'll never know unless we try. Gwen needs to see the reality of the home we've created here and how special it is. That may lead her to understand the importance of her role as the guardian of the Pendragon."

Lance and Artie exited the lighthouse, looking for any sign of Gwen. The spinning light from high above illuminated the area around them as it spun effortlessly into the night sky. The light darted across the water as the grassy knoll on top of the hill spread out before them. They spotted Gwen sitting on the ground near the edge of the cliff. She had her face buried in her knees as she sobbed uncontrollably. The boys rushed over to their friend and knelt, putting their hands on her shoulders to comfort her. The golden armor started to fade, twinkling in the evening sky as it disappeared from her arm.

"I didn't ask for this," she sobbed. "I don't want to be the guardian of the Pendragon. I want to be Gwen Iver—to go to school, graduate, then maybe college or travel and figure out my future. I'm not some savior or protector knight."

"Gwen, no one expects you to be anything but yourself," Lance said. "You need time to absorb all this and think things through."

"Yeah, and no matter what, we'll be here with you, Gwen. Lance and I will always be here for you." Artie's words comforted Gwen as she hung onto her two friends. They had forged a bond over the years of growing up together in Camelot Cove, and no matter the reality of their little town, they were not about to let it change their relationship.

Maude Reddy stood by the corner of the caretaker's house, peeking around the corner. She sneered while watching the two boys comfort Gwen, and it sickened her. She snuck up to the lighthouse, hoping to spy on Gwen and her friends, and it paid off. Maude saw and heard everything, from Gwen's golden arm to the talk about the

Pendragon. This was everything Morgan was waiting for; now, she could finally take down Gwen Iver for good.

# Chapter Four:

## *The Truth about Camelot Cove*

The alarm clock blared, and Gwen stirred from her slumber. She barely slept a wink that night as her mind still buzzed with a thousand questions. To top it off, her dreams were filled with images of the golden dragon and former wielders of the Pendragon, from her mother back to Queen Guinevere. It was like she had been reincarnated through history, reliving her past lives through the power of the Pendragon. This confused her even more, leaving Gwen with a terrible headache.

But none of that mattered. It was only her second day of school, and Gwen needed to get dressed and get to class. She looked at her arm, once covered in golden armor. It disappeared while she sat on the cliff with Lance and Artie. She wondered about it momentarily but put that thought out of her head as she climbed out of bed. With so much on her mind, Gwen quickly threw herself together, paying little attention to her appearance.

She stopped at the top of the stairs and gazed at the photos of her mother and father. The thought that someone murdered them for this power incensed her even more. Gwen wanted to find out who was responsible and make them pay for hurting her and her family. Only one person could tell her that—someone she did not want to talk to this morning, but she had no choice.

Gwen kissed her parents' images and walked down the stairs into the kitchen. Uncle Merle looked more normal than magical, cooking her breakfast. He was making pancakes, her favorite, but Gwen was not about to let the old man sway her. She was determined to get some answers this morning.

"Do you want some breakfast?" he asked, keeping his back to her while flipping the next batch of pancakes.

"Yes, please," Gwen said as she slowly took her seat at the table. Merle stacked a few of the freshly griddled pancakes on a plate, putting the rest on another before finally putting his spatula down and bringing the food to the table. He placed one plate in front of Gwen and the other in his seat as he sat down.

They sat quietly, not speaking a word as Merle began to butter his pancakes. "You better eat up before they get cold," he finally said, irritating Gwen even more. Before eating her breakfast, she started adding butter and syrup to her breakfast plate. As always, Uncle Merle's pancakes were tender and delicious. She wondered if he used magic to make them taste so good, but that was a question for another time.

"So, answer me this, Merlin," Gwen started to ask, but Merle held up his hand to immediately stop her.

"Rule number one, I don't answer to that name here, so don't call me that outside the cave. I'm Uncle Merle. I only answer to Merlin beneath the lighthouse, nowhere else."

Gwen continued to be irritated by the situation, but she knew if she wanted answers, she would have to play along. "Okay, Uncle Merle, do you know who murdered my parents?"

Merle finally looked at her. He seemed unsure, and Gwen wondered if he would lie to her. But that wouldn't help the old man. She wanted the truth, and she was determined to have it.

"I have suspicions but no evidence, except that I know magic was used to cause their accident."

"How do you know that?"

"Like any force of nature, magic leaves a residue that lingers behind over an affected area," Merle explained. "There was residue like that on your parents and what was left of the boat. It was declared an accident by the Coast Guard and other local authorities, but I know better. Someone killed them."

"But why would they kill them if they wanted to steal the Pendragon? That doesn't make sense."

"The problem was that the killer didn't realize your mother was driving the boat," Merle stated. "They went across the water to a restaurant in Marquette to celebrate their anniversary. However, your father had too much to drink, and your mother was driving the boat.

"The attack was meant to kill your father and incapacitate your mother, not the other way around," he continued. "When they discovered their mistake, they . . . they drowned your father, making sure that he couldn't expose their evil deeds."

Hearing that gave Gwen a chill but piqued her curiosity to know more. "But why do they want this?" Gwen motioned to her arm. "What good is it to them?"

"Like any power, Gwen, whether nuclear weapons and guns or magic and the Pendragon, it can be corrupted and abused. If the power of the Pendragon falls into the wrong hands, it could change the reality of the world as we know it."

"What do you mean?" Gwen asked, continuing to push Merle for more information. She could tell he was trying to sway her on the ways of magic and the Pendragon, but she was not easily convinced. He reached into his pocket and pulled out a match, striking it on the table to ignite the flame on the tip.

"Science is how the natural order of things operates in our world. For example, to create fire, you need fuel, oxygen, and a heat source, correct?" he explained as the flame flickered. "Magic bends the laws of science to change reality into whatever we want it to be." Merle waved his hand over the match, and the fire transformed into a fairy. The magical creature zipped around the kitchen until it burst over the table like fireworks on the Fourth of July.

"With the power of the Pendragon under their control, these deviants could transform the world into whatever they see fit. They would abuse power, not protect it. Would you want someone like Morgan Moor to possess power like that?"

Hearing that name incensed Gwen, and it begged the question. "Are you saying Morgan Moor was responsible for my parents' deaths?" Gwen asked. "Did she kill my mom and dad?"

Merle could see the anger swelling within her and tried to calm her down. "We don't know that for sure—"

"Don't lie to me!" She screamed, slamming her fist onto the table, but as she did, the armor suddenly appeared again, causing her to break the corner of the kitchen table, shattering the wood and dishes. Her anger turned to fear, realizing what the power of the Pendragon could do. She looked at Uncle Merle, obviously upset with her for abusing her abilities. He let out an audible sigh and shook his head, a simple way of letting the teenager know that she could not control this unearthly magic.

"You can't let your emotions flare out of control, Gwen," Merle cautioned. "The Pendragon reacts to your feelings, both good and bad. You have a lot to learn to control this power."

"I'm sorry about the table, Uncle Merle. I'll help you clean up this mess."

"I'll take care of this mess, yearling. Why don't you get going but stop by and see Viv on your way to school? She'll have some advice for you on controlling the Pendragon, among other things." Gwen closed her eyes and took a deep breath as she listened to Merle's advice and calmed down, causing the armor to fade again. She flexed her hand and arm as it returned to normal, still unsure about this power or even if she wanted it.

Gwen got up from the table and hurried off to gather her things for school. Merle looked at the mess scattered about the kitchen. "What a mess . . . I will need to invest in some spare furniture until she gets a handle on things."

Gwen hopped on her bike and raced down the coastline toward the piers. She got little to no answers from Uncle Merle, except he let slip that tidbit about Morgan Moor. *Is she behind my parents' deaths? Is she that desperate to kill someone so thoughtlessly?* Her mind raced with even more confusion, aside from the fact that she demolished the kitchen table with one blow. Maybe this Pendragon was good for something, especially if it meant revenge against her parent's killers.

Within minutes, Gwen reached the docks. She made a beeline for Viv's shack, ignoring the usual greetings from people walking about the boardwalk and the boats moored at the waterfront. The store was already open as Viv leaned across the counter, sipping a cup of coffee. In Gwen's mind, it was as if she was expecting her arrival.

"So, did you break anything else this morning?" Viv asked, smiling cheesily at the teenager.

Her announcement startled Gwen, who stopped short of the boat rental shack, frozen and surprised by Viv's question.

"How do you know about that?" she asked, feeling her heartbeat quicken.

"Oh, Gwen, I know a lot about many things. I can't share all my secrets with you, dear—not yet, at least." Gwen slid off her bike and walked over to the counter, thinking about what to say to Viv, but she spoke first. "Look, honey, I know you're upset with Merle and me, but we did this to protect you. It's how we've done it for thousands of years. The only difference is that normally, the torch is passed from mother to daughter. Your mom, God rest her soul, would have been the one to raise you and teach you about the Pendragon, but that was taken away from you, from us."

"Is it true what Merle said? Did Morgan Moor kill my parents?" Gwen asked, point blank. Viv sighed, letting Gwen know it was true, no matter how painful this was for her.

"We think so, but as Merle said, we can't prove it. Perhaps with the Pendragon in your hands, it may bring out the truth."

"But Morgan is only a year older than me. How can she be responsible for my parents' deaths?" Gwen asked, desperately trying to understand the situation.

"Morgan is a sorceress, a very old one. You may know her name from the legends—Morgana le Fay," Viv explained. Hearing the name of the mythical evil sorceress shocked Gwen even more than hearing she was related to King Arthur and Queen Guinevere.

"She's not immortal, like Merlin and I, but she can reincarnate her soul into a new body. She's done that for thousands of years, and every time, she's failed to get her hands on it, which is why you need to get the Pendragon under control." Viv poked a finger at Gwen for emphasis.

"I can't control this. I destroyed the kitchen table this morning!"

"Only because you haven't fully accepted the power. You can do so much more once you control those teenage hormones."

"Like what? Cast spells, hurl fireballs, and lightning bolts?" Gwen asked, curious as to what Viv meant. Viv scoffed at her assumptions.

"Don't believe everything you read in those ridiculous fantasy tropes," Viv asserted. "You're not a sorceress, so you don't cast spells. The Pendragon allows you to manipulate magic in its pure form, just like the Fae. It is a power beyond the human eye to see."

"Beyond the human eye? Viv, you're talking in riddles!" Gwen shouted, frustrated that she had not been given a straight answer. The old lady put down her coffee cup and stepped out from behind the counter. She took Gwen by the hand and led her to a large rainwater barrel sitting next to the shack on the pier.

"Summon the armor," Viv instructed.

Gwen looked at her arm and then back to Viv. "I don't know how to do that!"

"Calm your anger, little one, and think about the Pendragon as you saw it in the cave. Think about the sensation you felt when you touched it for the first time." Gwen looked at all the people scattered about the harbor, afraid to reveal this strange magic to them. "Don't worry about them. I know and trust everyone here. Now, focus on the armor."

Gwen closed her eyes and remembered how the armor felt on her arm: weightless and carefree, a soothing sensation when she touched the Pendragon in the cave. She opened her eyes and stared in amazement. Her hand glistened with magic; the golden armor glowed and encased her arm. It had been surprisingly easy to summon the armor.

"Now, reach into the water and splash it on your face, but keep your eyes closed until I tell you to open them," Viv instructed.

"But my makeup and my hair . . ." she argued after spending time getting ready for school. Viv shrugged her shoulders at the vanity of teenage girls.

"You can fix it before you head off to school. Now, do as you're told!"

Gwen did not argue anymore and scooped up some water with her armored hand and splashed it on her face. She kept her eyes closed as Viv carefully moved her around so she could look out over the area. "Now, open your eyes and witness the magic of the Fae." Gwen slowly opened her eyes, and when she did, she got the surprise of a lifetime.

The people she had seen every day in Camelot Cove were gone. The human forms that magically protected them from outsiders faded from view. She saw them as they were. Alongside the boats were mermen and mermaids, water sprites, selkies, naiads, and other sea creatures dancing about the cove. Gwen looked on the boardwalk and noticed witches, ogres, dryads, dwarves, elves, and other magical beings. Little fairies danced with sylphs through the air, swirling around the little community, sparkling off the glass of the many storefront windows. In the distance, she could see giants working in the lumber mill and the quarry on the outskirts of town. It was an incredible sight to see, and it filled Gwen with a newfound joy she never knew as she moved about the pier, taking it all in.

"Watch where you're going, Gwen, or you'll fall in the water," warned Oscar Peabody, Camelot Cove's harbor master. When Gwen twirled around, instead of the curmudgeonly old sea captain, she saw a dragon newt. His tiny, leathery wings flitted about as a lizard tail thumped the dock from beneath a long jacket. His old captain's hat was kept squarely on his head by horns curling like a ram's horns.

Gwen was startled at first, but then she realized who it was. "Sorry, Captain Peabody," she apologized before pausing and leaning in for a closer look. He stood still, not moving an inch, as Gwen circled him, careful not to step on his tail. "How do you get in and out of the boats with that cumbersome tail?"

Oscar was shocked when Gwen asked the question. Noticing the armor on her arm, he double-taked, looking at Viv. She held up her hand to ease his concerns. "It's okay, Oscar. She has the fairy sight now. She can see everything as it truly is."

Gwen heard the phrase "fairy sight" and looked over at Viv for the first time, which startled her even more. The old lady she had known all her life was gone. Instead, she saw a beautiful maiden covered in a shimmering gold dress, like her armor.

"Viv, are you? I mean, if Uncle Merle is Merlin, then you must be—"

"Yes, dear, I'm Vivienne, the Lady of the Lake." The facade soon faded as Viv transformed into her normal human appearance. "But let's just keep it simple between us, okay? I wouldn't want to confuse you more than you already are. Oscar, please let the others in the harbor know. We don't want to startle anyone else, given Gwen's stares."

Oscar gave a simple nod and turned to head down the pier, but not before he spun around to tell Gwen something. "And for your information, Gwen Iver, my tail is not cumbersome. It's muscular and easy to move, even for an old codger like me." He whipped his tail about as he said that, demonstrating his prowess.

"You're right, Captain Peabody. I'm sorry. I guess I have a lot to learn." She hoped her apology soothed the old sailor's heart as he tipped his hat politely before heading off.

"You're going to get a lot of stares, and I know you'll have a hundred and one questions, but for now, just get to school and enjoy the sights along the way. I'll let the rest of the folk know," Viv advised as she dragged her hand down Gwen's arm, causing the armor to fade again. "And you'll find a few surprises at school, too. Just act naturally and say nothing, especially to Morgan Moor or the Dreadmoor Gang. I'll take you around after school and reintroduce you to everyone, all right?"

Gwen held back a tear as her emotions got the best of her. She jumped up and hugged Viv. The gift of the fairy sight showed her so much about her little town. She started to realize how extraordinary it was here, and maybe the power of the Pendragon was worth protecting. She let Viv go and ran into the shack to use the mirror to fix her hair and makeup. Then, quickly, she hopped onto her bike and took off for school.

Viv watched her ride off, but not before waving toward a few fairies as they flew down, hovering next to her. "Go to the others and let them know Gwen has accepted the power of the Pendragon and the gift of fairy sight. I don't want anyone saying anything to her until I bring her around, understand?" The fairies squeaked in a high-pitched gibberish, their bodies flashing like stars in the night sky before they flitted and fluttered around town to warn everyone.

Viv momentarily worried, questioning whether giving Gwen the gift of fairy sight was wise. She would see things and more, but Viv hoped it would help her fully accept the power of the Pendragon. The future of Camelot Cove depended on it.

As Gwen rode through the town, her eyes were opened to the Fae's magic and beauty. Their presence was everywhere on the streets of Camelot Cove. People she saw daily showed their true colors through the gift of the fairy sight.

Edna McMullen kept such perfect plants in her garden shop because she was a dryad, a wood nymph who loved and cared for all living things. Her hair flowed like vines, feeding her the strength and beauty of the earth itself. An army of fauns, brownies, nymphs, and fairies helped her maintain the variety of plants under her care. From her little shop, the entire area seemed more "natural" than usual as plants and trees grew taller and spread like wildfire, connecting the buildings and homes across the community. It was in these areas that the smaller Fae creatures lived and thrived.

Everyone changed, including Rosina in her sweet shop. Gwen thought she was a great candymaker, but the fact that she was a witch attracting children with her sweets surprised her even more. Gerald Duffy, the scrawny general store owner, was a centaur, more than capable of easily handling heavy produce boxes. Stewart Eriksson and his wife, Sophia, jewelers from the Dragon's Treasure jewelry shop, were dwarves, craftsmen in all things gold and bejeweled.

The funniest thing Gwen noticed was that all the shops employed leprechauns as cashiers. These trickster spirits known for hoarding wealth excelled at finances and bookkeeping in the modern era, so their talents were widely used across town. Seeing all this helped her make sense of a strange yet wonderful community as Gwen quickly pedaled through it.

As she approached the school, Gwen noticed even more changes among her classmates. Ogres, gnomes, elves, dwarves, and various Fae races were mixed in with the human students of Camelot Cove High. She tried not to look around like Viv told her, but it was hard not to.

"Gwen, honey, you okay?" Triss asked, startling Gwen. As she turned around to look at her friend, she saw changes in her, too. Triss was dressed as stylish as always, but her long, pointed ears protruded from the side of her head. The piercings extended up her ears, from the lob to the pointy tip. Gwen could not believe that one of her best friends was an elf.

"Yeah, I'm fine," Gwen said, swallowing hard so as not to say anything unusual. Triss, however, was far more intelligent than that and realized something was wrong with her friend. She looked at Gwen closely, examining every part of her, even moving inches from her face, until it hit her.

"You can see me, can't you?" she said, but Gwen tried to play it cool.

"Of course, I can. You're standing right in front of me."

"You know damn well what I mean, Gwen Iver," Triss said, flicking her finger off her pointed ear. Gwen desperately tried not to stare, but she couldn't help herself. "You opened the box, didn't you? You've got the fairy sight!"

Gwen did not want to say anything out loud, so she nodded. Triss breathed a sigh of relief as she reached out and hugged her friend. Gwen was shocked at her reaction.

"Oh, thank Arduinna," Triss exclaimed before releasing her. "I don't have to hide from you anymore. You inherited the power of the Pendragon."

"Wait, you knew about this too? Why didn't you tell me?"

"Because when my parents showed me who I was, I had to swear never to expose my true nature to anyone outside the Fae. Most humans don't learn the truth until they are adults, and some never do. Only the guardian of the Pendragon was entrusted with our secret, and until you accept the power, I couldn't tell you about any of it."

Gwen understood why, especially after seeing the town in all its glory, but Triss was more concerned with how she looked to her friend. "So, what do you think?" she asked, posing for her. "I look even better as an elf than a human girl, don't I?"

Gwen could not help but laugh, agreeing wholeheartedly with her assessment. "Yes, you do, but I think you would be stylish no matter what you wear or how you look."

"I know, but honestly, I get jealous of those cosplay girls stealing my look. I could give them a run for their money."

The two laughed as they spied Artie and Lance riding up to park their bikes. Gwen feared that after last night, they would be worried about Gwen and rush to school as soon as possible. Seeing her laughing alongside Triss seemingly eased their concerns. The elf, however, tugged on Gwen's blouse, worried about something entirely different.

"They don't know, do they?" Triss queried.

"About the Pendragon, yes. They helped me figure out the puzzle box," Gwen explained. "But they don't know anything about the Fae other than they exist in Camelot Cove."

"Okay, so my secret's safe for the time being," Triss bellowed, sighing relief. Gwen realized her friend did not want to be put on display before anyone. "I know Artie would have a thousand questions for me."

"A thousand and one," Gwen joked, as the two laughed. Artie and Lance parked their bikes in the rack before they strolled over to Gwen and Triss. They both looked like they wanted to ask direct questions, but not with Triss here.

"Are you okay, Gwen? You were pretty shaken up last night," Lance inquired.

"Yeah, but it's nothing a good night's sleep couldn't cure," Gwen remarked brightly. "I'm fine, guys; really, I am."

"Of course you are, Gwen, honey," Triss added, hugging her friend across her shoulders as they walked toward the entrance. "It's only the second day of school. We've got a whole year ahead of us."

# Chapter Five:

# Morgan and Maude

Gwen had to control her emotions all day as she wandered Camelot Cove High School. The array of unique individuals roaming the school grounds, from the teachers and staff to the students, continued to surprise her. She relied on Triss to help her occasionally identify the various races that wandered about. From a succubus as the school nurse to a faun as the PE teacher, it was an eye-opening experience for Gwen.

During lunch, Gwen ate with Triss to get more information on the surroundings, notably the Dreadmoor

Gang. It seemed they were the worst of the worst. It seemed they were the worst of the worst. They were an assortment of legendary monsters, too—a minotaur, an ogre, a Lamia, and a harpy. Morgan Moor and Maude Reddy seemed to be the only humans in the group.

While discussing some differences among the various Fae around them, they were interrupted by Principal Andhra Cornelius. Gwen always thought he was a bit snobbish, always looking down at the students, and now she knew why. Principal Cornelius was a vanara, a human-sized monkey with superior intelligence. Even with a three-piece button-down suit, his ape-like hands, feet, and tail covered in a thin layer of soft fur were evident.

"Miss Iver, Miss Paul, a word, please," he said in a prim and proper tone. The girls got up from the table and followed him across the lunchroom for a more private chat.

"Yes, Principal Cornelius? Is there something wrong?" Gwen asked as he leaned in to whisper to them.

"I understand that this is all new to you, Miss Iver, but I suggest you do your sightseeing after school and not draw attention to yourself by gawking at every Fae that walks by your table." Gwen was shocked to hear him speak to her so directly. "And you should know better, Miss Paul," he scolded Triss. "There is a time and a place for this sort of behavior. You two should be focused on your classes, not telling the difference between a satyr and a faun."

"How did you know?" Gwen asked quietly.

"Lady Vivienne sent out the word that the Pendragon came into her own," he explained. "Now, besides being responsible for a mixture of human and Fae children, I have to keep an eye on the Pendragon, too. Not that I mind doing that, but it would help if you didn't attract so much attention to yourself right now."

"Yes, sir, sorry, Principal Cornelius," Gwen apologized. Triss added her apology before the principal straightened his glasses and shooed the girls back to their table. Gwen spotted a hint of giddiness from the normally stoic school principal. It seemed he enjoyed being able to exercise his authority over the wielder of the Pendragon, something he would relish in the years to come.

When they returned to their seats, Artie, Lance, and G Wayne also joined them at the table. It was the first time Gwen saw G Wayne with the same elf characteristics as his sister. He did, however, have custom EarPods that attached comfortably to his extended ears. His priorities were more form and function, not style like his sister's. Gwen did her best not to stare as she sat back down to finish her lunch.

"What did the principal want?" Artie curiously asked. Gwen stumbled to find a simple explanation, but Triss swooped in and saved her from further exposing her secrets.

"He was asking if Gwen was going to run for any student council positions in the upcoming elections," Triss lied quite convincingly. "He heard that she was the middle school vice president, and he hoped to have a diverse representation from all the classes." Expounding on the truth convinced the boys not to press the issue further. Gwen, however, realized that Triss may have accidentally boxed her into running for a seat on the student council.

"My, my . . . There's something different about you, Gwen," Morgan stated seductively as she walked by the table. Maude followed close behind as they carried their lunch trays, looking for a place to sit in the cafeteria. "I can't place my finger on it, but there is something rather stunning in your aura. A new haircut, perhaps?"

Maude giggled at the joke, but not Gwen, as her blood boiled. "No, nothing new, Morgan. I'm just beginning to see things as they truly are. You know who your friends are compared to the snakes in the grass." Although her statement was quite ordinary to everyone else, Gwen saw that Morgan knew exactly what she meant.

An irritated Maude lunged at Gwen, daring to challenge Morgan outright, but Artie's wicked stepsister stepped between the girls, stopping Maude from doing anything rash. "You need to be careful of those snakes, Gwen darling. They can bite you when you least expect it." She smiled a sly grin. "Artie, be a darling little brother and pick up my dry cleaning after school for me? I have something urgent to attend to, and I don't think I'll make it to Mr. Brave's shop before it closes. Would you please be a dear?"

Artie scoffed at his stepsister, putting him on the spot like that. Gwen could see he did not want to be a jerk about it, especially in front of everyone. He had no choice but to give in to her. "Sure, I don't mind," he said. With a wink and a smile, Morgan left them behind to join her friends for lunch. Maude smirked at them before turning to join Morgan.

"Why do you do that, Artie? Give in to her?" G Wayne asked.

"It's easier than arguing with her. Morgan has a way of twisting things around to make it your fault if you don't do what she asks."

"That doesn't make it right, Artie," Gwen said. "Someone needs to bring her down a peg or two."

"Maybe someday, Gwen, but let's worry about that another day," Lance interrupted. "I'll take you to see Viv after school while Artie runs his errand. You can meet us there before we take Gwen home. Sound good?"

Artie acknowledged Lance's plan, but Gwen could plainly see the anguish on his face as he tried to bury it deep inside rather than let it show. Maybe once she fully accepted the power of the Pendragon, she could make his life a little easier. *But then again, perhaps this is something he must figure out alone.* Gwen struggled with her dilemma. *He'll never come out from under Morgan's shadow if he doesn't stand up to her.*

The bell rang, and another day ended at Camelot Cove High. Artie took off to finish his errand for Morgan while Lance rode off in the opposite direction with Gwen toward the harbor. They would meet up again later once he finished running around after his stepsister.

Artie sped through the streets of Camelot Cove on his bike, racing to reach Mr. Brave's Tailor and Dry Cleaning as quickly as possible. He needed to pick up Morgan's clothes, rush them home, and then meet up with Gwen at the docks. There was no time to waste.

He could not even begin to fathom how dizzying the past 24 hours had been for Gwen. She had so much to cope with between school, homework, Morgan Moor and her gang, and now the power of the Pendragon. Artie wanted to be there for Gwen, no matter what.

As usual, Morgan neglected to tell him how much he had to pick up. She had dropped off dozens of skirts, blouses, and dresses at the cleaners. The hanging garments overloaded him. "Need a hand, Artie?" Artie looked out from behind a load of plastic-covered bundles to see Percy Perry strolling toward him. The middle schooler fancied Artie as a mentor.

He was short for his age—a little over four feet tall—and his skinny body, bushy brown hair, and freckles resembled Artie in many ways, except for their hobbies. Artie was a ravenous reader, while Percy enjoyed mechanics. He loved tinkering with little machines, studying how they worked, and turning them into fun toys.

"Hey Percy, no, I'm good. Besides, I wouldn't want you getting in trouble with Morgan if you drop or wrinkle her clothes," Artie said as he struggled with the clothes and his bike.

"Well, at least let me push your bike for you. That way, you can carry those clothes without any problem." Percy took control of Artie's bike, and the two walked side-by-side through the streets. "Boy, that stepsister of yours runs you ragged, doesn't she?"

"Yeah, but what can I do? Either she gets mad and complains to my stepdad, and his anger is worse than hers." Percy nodded, shrugging his shoulders for Artie. The stepchild knew full well how stern the sheriff of Camelot Cove could be. He had the bruises from those occasional whippings meant to keep him in line.

"Why didn't she pick them up herself? I saw Morgan and the rest of her gang heading toward your house right after school." Percy's revelation surprised Artie. He should have guessed this was just one of Morgan's dirty tricks.

"Well, do me a favor, Percy, and put my bike in the garage for me," Artie said. "If Morgan's at the house, I don't want you getting any piece of her fury." Artie convinced Percy to avoid the wrath of his twisted stepsister, as the middle schooler received many an evil look from Morgan just for being Artie's friend.

The two boys finally reached the house on the outskirts of town. It was a luxurious two-story home for such a small family, but Morgan would not have it any other way. She occupied the largest room—even more prominent than her father's—with a private bathroom and ample closet space. At the same time, Artie was relegated to the smallest room in the house, down in the basement, far away from his stepsister and her excessive ways.

Percy parked the bike in the garage while Artie headed up the steps into the house. He could barely see as he walked into the house and suddenly felt the garments being grabbed from his hands. He was shoved and slapped, causing his glasses to fly off his face and bounce across the floor. When he regained his composure and got to his feet, Artie finally realized what was happening—an ambush.

Members of the Dreadmoor Gang stood about the living room. Morgan sat comfortably in an overstuffed easy chair while Maude stood behind her, grinning a wicked smile with her yellow-stained teeth. The others were scattered about the room, blocking any chance of escape. Otis, the largest member, stood over him, delicately holding the dry cleaning.

"Prunella, be a dear and hang those clothes in my closet for me before Otis wrinkles them any more than they already are," Morgan ordered. The pig-tailed blonde carefully relieved Otis of the garments and took them away before Morgan turned her attention to Artie.

"I thought you had urgent business after school, Morgan, not lounging around with your gang," Artie said, incensed at his stepsister sending him off on needless errands.

"I do have urgent business, Arthur, with you. I just needed to get you away from your little friends." Morgan motioned to Otis, at which the muscle-bound brute pushed Artie toward Morgan and forced him to stand before her. Reluctantly, he had no choice but to comply. "Now, little brother, tell me everything you know about the Pendragon."

Artie could not believe what Morgan asked. He had only learned about this ancient power last night. *How does she know about the Pendragon?* He wondered what to do but decided to play it cool. "Pendragon? What's that, a new hot sauce? Or is it some new dance craze, like dubstep?"

A couple of the Dreadmoor Gang laughed at Artie's joke. Morgan glared at them, causing them to stop laughing immediately. Maude wanted to beat the answers out of him, clenching her fists so tight that her nails cut into her palms. Morgan glared at her protégé, causing Maude to unclench her fists.

"You know exactly what it is, Artie. Maude saw you and sweet little Lance hovering over the little princess last night outside the lighthouse. I'm sure Merlin took you into his secret underground grotto and explained *EVERYTHING* to you. I need to know where the power was stored before Gwen accepted the Pendragon for herself. You had to be there when it happened; otherwise, Merlin wouldn't have let you in on the secret."

"You're out of your mind, Morgan. I have no idea what you're talking about."

"Really? Then perhaps I should show you," Morgan said before she picked up a bottle of water on the table next to her and poured a little into her hand. She brought it to her mouth and blew softly across the water as blue flecks of magic sparkled like glitter from her breath. Before Artie could say anything, she threw the water in his face. He closed his eyes, wiping the water away with his fingers. When he opened them, he suddenly saw what Merlin said about the Fae living amongst them in Camelot Cove.

Artie looked around the room and saw the Dreadmoor Gang as their true selves. Otis was an ogre, massive and uglier than his human disguise, with light green skin, horns, and tusks jutting from his jaw. Prunella was a Lamia—a snake woman—with a human torso and a snake-like lower body. Titus, a minotaur, and Cecilia, a harpy, cuddled beside each other on the sofa as fur and feathers intertwined. It was a menagerie of magical creatures that Artie only imagined from storybooks and movies.

Even more shocking, he suddenly realized that Morgan did something to the water to make him see all this—something magical and unexpected. *Is she some kind of sorceress?* His concern for Gwen grew as he pondered the arcane abilities of his stepsister. Morgan, however, became even more intimidating as she leaned into her stepbrother.

"You don't seem too surprised, Artie. The old man must have told you about the Fae in Camelot Cove."

"Yeah, he did," Artie shot back at her. "He also said there were those in Camelot Cove who wanted to steal the power of the Pendragon for themselves. I should have expected it to be you and your gang of reprobates."

"Steal it? Oh no, Artie, you have it all wrong," Morgan eloquently explained. "You can't steal the Pendragon. It must be relinquished willingly; otherwise, you can't control or contain the power."

"And you expect Gwen to just give it to you?"

"Oh, don't worry about the little lost princess, Artie. That's unimportant right now. First, I need the container the Pendragon was kept in. I can't risk losing it again."

As soon as Morgan said that, Artie knew precisely what she meant. The story Merlin told them about Gwen's parents being murdered for the Pendragon. Morgan was involved, somehow. Artie clenched his fists as his blood boiled at the thought of his stepsister being a murderer. The rage boiled within Artie, and Morgan reveled in it, like sipping a fine wine.

Artie went to punch his sister, but Morgan caught his hand in midair, not with her hand but with magic. Her fingers danced about, containing his fist in a magical field. The air around his hand sparkled with the same magic she breathed into the water. He could not move it, no matter how hard he struggled against her. Morgan delighted in seeing Artie squirm beneath her power.

"I know you have plenty of questions, Arthur, but we can save that for later. I want you to tell me about the container for the Pendragon. What was it, and where can I find it?"

Artie continued to fight against her power, even though he knew it was pointless. Still, he was not about to give in to her whims. "I won't tell you anything!" he said defiantly.

Morgan grew increasingly frustrated as Artie seemingly laughed in her face. She was used to getting her way on everything, and yet he continued to resist her. Luckily, Morgan had other means of making him talk.

"Oh yes, you will, Artie. Yes, you will!" Morgan released his hand and nodded over at Prunella. The Lamia slithered behind Artie and grabbed his arms, pinning them against his sides. She was stronger than she appeared. She bared a pair of long fangs dripping with toxins. Artie winced in pain as Prunella bit his shoulder, injecting him with the powerful drug.

As the neurotoxin flowed through his bloodstream, his mind began to fall into a haze. Morgan watched carefully until the desired effects set in and nodded for Prunella to release him. Artie collapsed onto his knees in front of Morgan, unable to move or speak, his eyes glazed over, his mind falling into a dense fog.

Morgan lifted his chin so she could look into his eyes. Artie could not react or fight back against her or understand how or why this was happening to him. "Don't struggle,

Arthur, not that you can. The poison secreted by Prunella's fangs is a paralytic toxin, but they act like a truth serum. In the old days, the Lamia would subdue parents with their bite so they could steal their children and eat them."

Prunella made a puking motion, sticking her finger in her mouth to show her disdain for the old ways. "Fortunately, Prunella and the rest of her kind have abstained from that horrible practice. Still, their venom is quite potent when necessary," she continued before she smacked Artie across the face to get his attention. "Now then, my darling stepbrother, where is the container for the Pendragon?"

Arthur stammered and murmured, unable to fight against Morgan. "A box in the kitchen," he said. "Merle put it on a shelf over the stove."

"A box? What kind of box?" Morgan inquired.

"It was a puzzle box with Viking runes on the slats. Gwen couldn't figure out how to open it, so I helped her."

"You're always the resourceful bookworm, aren't you, Artie?" Morgan joked, but the idea of this puzzle box concerned her. The rest of the gang became confused over something so simple.

"What is it, Morgan? Cecelia and I can go get it and be out of there before the old lighthouse keeper suspects anything," Maude gloated to her.

"That doesn't worry me, Maude. I can run circles around that old man. It's the puzzle box that concerns me. If the power of the Pendragon goes back into the box, it'll be nearly impossible to open and take it. We must get little Gwen to return the Pendragon to the box and keep it unlocked. Otherwise, I'll have to wait another generation to obtain the power."

"We can't let little Miss Priss hang onto that power," Maude argued. "The longer she has it, the more powerful she'll become."

"Maude, you need to control that hatred for Gwen Iver," Morgan admonished her protégé. "Rage like yours will only cloud your mind to your true purpose."

"Trust me, Morgan, my mind is clear when it comes to Gwenie-poo," Maude interrupted, something she rarely did with Morgan. "That little brat took everything from me. She is going to get everything she deserves in spades."

Morgan grabbed Maude by the hand, twisting it painfully to get her attention. "Just as long as I get what I want first. After that, you can do whatever you like to Gwen Iver. Do you understand me?" Maude nodded her head violently until Morgan let her go. She shook her hand vigorously until the pain faded away.

"How DO we get the little princess to do what you want? We don't even know how powerful she is with the Pendragon." Maude wondered. Morgan grinned as she stared down at Artie.

"We need to test little Gwen to see what she's capable of. And to do that, you need the right bait to lure her in. We need to visit the Cypress Grove Cemetery."

Percy watched and listened from the window as Morgan plotted her next move with the rest of her gang. He knew exactly what happened to Artie because he was one of the

Fae—a gnome. His industrious nature and small stature were true to form for his kind. Percy cherished his friendship with Artie because he treated him as an equal, unlike the other Fae, who often looked down on him.

Percy worried what Morgan and her gang might do to his friend. He knew the only person who could save Artie was Gwen Iver, the Pendragon. There was no time to waste as the little gnome slipped away.

# Chapter Six:

## *A Grim Reception*

Gwen enjoyed her walk around the harbor and boardwalk, accompanied by Viv. It was as if she was getting to know her hometown again. The sights, sounds, and people were completely different, as was their attitude toward Gwen. She had always been cordial with the townspeople, but somehow it was different now. The newfound power of the Pendragon brought with it respect and admiration for her taking on the responsibility of such a prestigious role.

It was strange for the teenager to interact with such beings as elves, dwarfs, mermaids, and the like—a menagerie usually seen in movies and fairy tales. Gwen was happy to have Viv with her on this tour. Some of the Fae were creatures straight out of nightmares in their appearance. Still, they were regular folk in how they acted and carried out their everyday life—the years of living together in Camelot Cove turned these terrifying monsters into a simple community in everything they did.

Gwen absorbed everything about the diverse nature of the Fae from Viv. Their unique nature, abilities, and cultural sensitivities were explained in explicit detail so she could better understand her role as the Pendragon. Viv explained that all this was done to protect the Fae from the corruptive influences of the human world and themselves.

"While Merle and I protect Camelot Cove from the outside world's influences, the Pendragon protects the Fae," Viv said during their walkabout.

"Protect them from who? Humans? Outsiders?"

"From themselves!" she added emphatically. "There are still ancient animosities between the races of the Fae and humans. The conflicts vary, so Merle and I try to stay out of it, negotiating where we can, but it's up to the Pendragon to enforce the laws of the Fae."

"The laws? Like a policeman?"

"No, the ancient laws laid down from the dawn of the Fae. The Pendragon ensures those laws are adhered to. Otherwise, there will be nothing but chaos. Then, the human world will be dragged into our conflict, and the result would mean the end of our way of life."

Gwen loved history and mythology. She listened intently to the stories of all these races coming together to form the community known as Camelot Cove. "So, these laws, what are they?" Gwen asked as they continued their walkabout.

"There are only three . . . Number one, no Fae will harm a human, and no human will harm a Fae. Many races once hunted humans as prey, but that would have brought undue attention to our community.

"Number two, respect each culture within the Fae and do not interfere in them. These ancient customs date back to the dawn of time and are not to be interrupted unless they break rule number one.

"And number three, never reveal the secret of the Fae or Camelot Cove. Any Fae or human that does will be exiled from Camelot Cove forever," Viv concluded.

"Exiled? How does that work exactly? Don't you risk more people finding out if you send Fae or humans away from their homes? Their families?"

"Humans are stripped of their memories as part of their exile so as not to reveal the true nature of Camelot Cove," Viv explained. "For the Fae, they are sent out into the world, forced to wander and live in the shadows, seen but unseen."

"But that's impossible. We would have seen or heard about others if they lived outside the protection of the cove," Gwen argued.

"Oh, you've heard of them—Bigfoot, the Abominable Snowman, the Loch Ness Monster, the Jersey Devil, the

Chupacabra, and more," Viv explained. "All of these different sightings from around the world are exiled Fae."

The extreme measures took Gwen aback, but Viv assured her this was necessary. "I know it seems radical to you, Gwen dear, but I assure you it is something we do as a last resort. After the first few times of enforcing the exile rule, many of the Fae have worked hard to keep our secret safe. We have evolved with the modern times, using every means necessary to keep our secret."

"What do you mean?" Gwen asked.

"In some areas, we've combined magic with technology to keep our secret. All the tiny Fae creatures—fairies, brownies, sprites, and the like—are networked across the entire community. Nothing happens in Camelot Cove that they don't know about.

"Plus, your friends—Triss and G Wayne—their family runs a security firm here in Camelot Cove, but in reality, they protect our secret," Viv continued. "Elves excel in surveillance. They use magical and electronic countermeasures to keep an eye on the entire town while using complicated algorithms to search the web for any mention of Fae concerning Camelot Cove, erasing them from the internet."

Gwen could not believe how complex their security was in what she considered a sleepy little town on the edge of nowhere. With all the precautions, it was no wonder their secret had remained safe all these years. However, there was something that still troubled Gwen and the responsibility of the Pendragon.

"Viv, one thing I still don't understand," Gwen began. "If there's all this surveillance—electronic and magical network—all across the town, how does Morgan and her Dreadmoor Gang get away with all their shenanigans?"

"I told you, Gwen honey, Morgan is a powerful sorceress in her own right. She uses her magic to avoid detection at all costs. Plus, with her father as sheriff and on the city council, he always sides with her. Until she gets caught, Morgan Moor will continue to do as she pleases. Only when you fully accept the power of the Pendragon will you be able to stop her evil intentions."

"I still don't understand what you mean by that," Gwen snapped, her tone rather frustrated with the Lady of the Lake. "I'm already wearing the armor. What more is there to accept about the ridiculous Pendragon thingy?"

"That attitude right there is why you don't understand," Viv stated as she stepped in front of Gwen, poking her finger into the teenager. "The Pendragon is not ridiculous. It's a responsibility. The armor is just a manifestation, not the power itself. The magic resides in here." She tapped Gwen's heart with her finger, making her point. "Magic makes the impossible possible, as long as you believe in it, but because you haven't fully accepted the responsibility of the Pendragon, you don't have access to the full power at your disposal."

"What if I don't? What happens if I don't accept it and don't become the Pendragon?"

"Then the power will return to the box and wait for the next heir," Viv explained. "If that happens, the chaos after your mother died will rise again, maybe worse this time."

"What do you mean? What happened after Mom died?" Gwen asked, curious to learn more about what happened to her parents. Before Viv could respond, Percy ran up to them, out of breath. It was the first time Gwen had seen the middle schooler in his proper form as a gnome. It took her a minute to realize who he was.

"Percy Perry, is that you?" Gwen asked, but Percy dropped to one knee before he could answer. He bowed his head and crossed his arms across his chest as a sign of reverence to the Pendragon.

"Please, my Lady of the Pendragon, I need your help," he implored. Gwen was confused by the little gnome prostrating before her. She looked at Viv to hopefully understand why he acted that way.

"The gnomes have always revered the Pendragon since your ancestor saved them from an inebriated manticore running amok," Viv explained. Gwen could not believe that they admired her just because of her ancestor. She reached down and tilted Percy's chin so he looked directly at her.

"Percy, it's me, Gwen. We've known each other for years. You don't need to bow down to me," she said as she took his hands and helped him to his feet. "Now, what's wrong?"

Percy took a deep breath as he collected his thoughts. Gwen thought he might be conflicted by everything his family taught him about the Pendragon and being a friend to Gwen. "Morgan Moor and her gang tricked Artie into telling them about you and the Pendragon." He continued to explain everything he saw and heard from outside the house. Every word turned to anger in Gwen as the rage against Morgan Moor built.

"Where are they taking him, Percy?" Gwen interjected, grabbing the boy by his shoulders.

"I heard them say something about the Cypress Grove Cemetery. Morgan wants them to determine how much of the Pendragon is under your control."

"Viv, warn Uncle Merle they're after the puzzle box. I'm going after Artie."

Gwen started to walk away with Percy, but Viv stopped her. "You can't face down Morgan Moor alone—not yet!"

"You want me to take on this responsibility, so I'm going to use it to save my friend," she snapped at Viv. "I will not let that woman think she can get away with whatever she wants anymore."

Suddenly, Lance rode up on his bike, seemingly bewildered by Gwen's fury and Artie's absence. "What's going on? Where's Artie?" he asked.

"Morgan tricked him into running her errands to separate us so she could find out about the Pendragon," Gwen said. Her outburst caught Lance off guard, especially with Percy around.

"Gwen, are you sure you should be saying that with certain people around?" Lance whispered.

Gwen realized that even though Lance knew about the Fae, he could not see them without the fairy sight she possessed. She summoned her armor, scooped up some water as before, and threw it into Lance's face. He spat out the water, rubbing his eyes.

"Geez, Gwen, what did you do . . . that . . . for?" He stuttered as he opened his eyes and saw the truth about

Camelot Cove for the first time. He gawked at everything around him, spinning in a circle as he realized the truth of what Merlin had told them.

"Gwen Iver, you cannot give anyone you want the gift of fairy sight! There are rules and protocols about these things!" Viv yelled at her.

"Lance already knew about the Fae and me, and he is one of the few people in this town I trust implicitly. If you want me to be the Pendragon, I will start making my own decisions," she shot back before grabbing her bike. "Percy, you ride with Lance. Let's go!"

Percy climbed nimbly onto Lance's handlebars as they rode off after Gwen as she quickly pedaled toward the cemetery on the outskirts of town. She stormed away with a fury never seen in the teenager before. Viv cursed under her breath at the reckless nature of Gwen's youth, but deep down, she was happy to see her come into her own.

*Maybe this will make her fully integrate with the Pendragon, but it's too dangerous for her to go it alone.* Viv tapped her foot against a stone footing where the boardwalk met the pier. A pair of eyes opened from within the stone and looked up at her.

"Tell the Spriggans to keep an eye on Cypress Grove Cemetery and help the Pendragon should the need arise," she said. The eyes blinked twice, then closed, forming back into the rock. Viv needed to warn Merle about Morgan Moor's maneuverings against the Pendragon. She had to trust Gwen and her friends to see this through.

The trio raced through the streets, with Gwen leading the way and Lance trailing behind. Gwen looked back to see what was keeping them. Lance looked around awkwardly as all the new sights and sounds seemingly overwhelmed him. Thanks to the fairy sight, he was really seeing things in his hometown for the first time.

"Watch where you're going, Lance!" Percy warned him to keep his eyes on the road, but even that distracted Lance. Gwen could hear them bantering about Percy's secret life as one of the Fae.

"So, how old are you really, Percy? Aren't magical beings like you older than you appear?" Lance inquired.

"I'm only twelve years old, dummy. We still start our lives the same as you humans. We only live a lot longer," Percy explained sarcastically to his human friend. "My grandmother is 670 years old."

"Grandma Betty? Really? Wow, you wouldn't know it by looking at her."

"Can we do ancestry research another time? We need a plan to get Artie away from the Dreadmoor Gang," Gwen snapped at them.

"We have a bigger problem than the Dreadmoor Gang, Gwen. As night approaches, the cemetery is about to be filled with various dark Fae," Percy explained.

"Like what, Percy?"

"Banshees, Will O' the Wisps, Barghests, ghouls, church grims, Dullahan, you name it," he responded. "Most of us stay away from the cemeteries at night. It can get pretty scary, even for the Fae."

"Will they attack us?" Lance questioned.

"As long as we're with the Pendragon, no. If we stick close to Gwen, we should be okay." Percy's words were not as comforting to Gwen, but none of that mattered. She had to save Artie from that twisted witch, Morgan, and her gang. "One last thing," Percy interjected. "Whatever you do, Lance, don't attack. Let them take the first swing."

"Why? If we can surprise them, striking first is always easiest."

"Yes, but not when it comes to the Fae," Percy countered. "If you attack a Fae, it's seen as a human exerting their dominance over our kind, and the Fae don't like that. Why do you think your dad never fights back against Mr. Dennison?"

"Walter Dennison? The owner of the Viking Table restaurant? I mean, he and Dad argue over everything from the loading zone behind the hotel to the noise coming from the restaurant during late-night parties," Lance recalled. "It always seemed like they were on the verge of blows, but my father never raised a hand to him."

"That's because Mr. Dennison is a troll, which is why you only see him at his restaurant at night or on overcast, rainy days," Percy interjected. "He always argues with your father, no matter how big or small the issue, knowing full well that if he ever struck Mr. Dennison intentionally, your dad would be in big trouble."

"Wow, that makes perfect sense now," Lance laughed. "I remember when I raised a fist at Mr. Dennison, but my father stopped me. I guess I'll have to be a little more cautious around him. That's good to know, Percy, but doesn't that mean the Fae can do whatever they want to humans like me?"

"Rule number one, no Fae will harm a human, and no human will harm a Fae. That balance is what keeps everyone in line, right, Percy?" Gwen interjected. Percy nodded his head repeatedly. "It may be prudent to allow the Fae to strike first because the punishment against them is probably far more stringent than it is for a human."

"Correct, my Lady of the Pendragon. There are far more dire consequences for any Fae reverting to their old ways to wage war against humankind."

Lance looked at Gwen, bemused after hearing Percy's new name for her. "My Lady of the Pendragon?"

"Don't ask," she coaxed, hoping he would forget what Percy said as the trio pulled up to the cemetery. The last rays of the sun disappeared over the tree line, and the sky turned black, revealing a veil of stars.

Cypress Grove lived up to its name as rows of majestic cypress trees lined the road leading up to the cemetery. The stone walls of this ancient burial site—used for centuries since the founding of Camelot Cove—looked even more foreboding in the dark. The mausoleums, crypts, and statues filling the cemetery made navigating through the crowded graveyard on bikes challenging.

As the three entered the cemetery, Lance and Gwen left their bikes near the gate. Gwen was a little apprehensive, but she desperately wanted to find Artie. On the other hand, Percy led the way in without hesitation. "Come on. I know my way around. I visit this place all the time," he said with glee.

Gwen had a renewed appreciation for the little gnome. She knew Percy was an intelligent kid, but he was gutsy too. "Hold on, Percy. We need some light. This place is way too dark."

"Perhaps I can be of assistance," came a soft voice from a nearby tombstone. The three looked to see a little cloaked figure sitting casually on the grave marker. A blue ember burned brightly from within the hood. "Welcome to Cypress Grove. It is an honor for a simple Will O' the Wisp to address the Pendragon."

"Will O' the Wisp?" Lance inquired, examining the petite Fae with increased curiosity.

"I was not addressing you, human boy! Know your place!"

"Hey, he's with me, okay? No need to be so rude!" Gwen snapped back.

"My apologies, Gwen Iver. I meant no disrespect." The Fae apologized with a courteous bow. "I should have realized that the Pendragon would have knights to accompany her."

"Don't worry about Eustis; he's harmless," Percy explained. "Will O' the Wisps no longer lure humans to their death off the beaten path. Now, they merely act as a guide through the darkness for the people of Camelot Cove."

"Come now, Percy, you make me sound a trite blasé. Where's the fun in that?"

"Come on, Eustis. We need your help. The Dreadmoor Gang has our friend, Artie, somewhere in the graveyard. Do you know where?" Percy asked.

"Oh yeah, those idiots. They're over in the back corner, near the grave of Tituba, the first Salem witch. Be careful with that lot. They're a bunch of crazy buggers."

"You don't have to tell us that. The question is, how do we find our way through the darkness?" Gwen asked. "You can't see anything in there."

"Well, allow me to serve the Pendragon. Summon your armor and reach under my hood," Eustis told Gwen. She hesitated initially but remembered something she had heard on her tour around the cove with Viv—trust. *Trust must exist between humans and Fae for our community to exist.*

Gwen summoned the armor and reached her hand into the blue flame under the hood of the Wil O' the Wisp. When she pulled her hand back, the bright blue flame now encircled it with a soft glow of firelight. She was amazed at the abilities she was gaining through the Pendragon. The more Gwen used this incredible power, the stronger it bonded to her soul.

"Thank you for your help, Eustis. I appreciate your gift," Gwen thanked the tiny Fae, who bowed at the gratitude. "Let's go. Percy, you lead the way."

The three friends moved into the graveyard, finding their way by the flame of the Will O' the Wisp powered by the Pendragon. Percy guided them past the monuments, statues, and ornamentation. Along the way, they saw some of the other Fae that Percy mentioned before emerging from their daily slumber to explore the night. Some of them were the stuff of nightmares, looking as dark and malevolent as the stories about them. However, as Percy predicted, they kept their distance from the Pendragon.

Soon, Percy slowed his pace as they approached the grave of Tituba, but no one was there. The tomb and the area around it were empty. Lance seemed disappointed to discover the Dreadmoor Gang was missing.

"Geez, I guess that little wisp lied, leading us on a wild goose chase."

"No way, Eustis is a good Fae," Percy argued. "He gives the best tours of the famous people buried in the cemetery." Gwen stared at the empty gravesite and wondered if there was another possibility.

"Or maybe they're hiding from us," she considered, staring at the flame burning around her fingertips. "Viv said that 'magic makes the impossible possible,' so maybe I could use it to my advantage."

Gwen extended her hand and visualized the flame spreading over the entire area, burning away any lingering magic. Suddenly, the fire shot out from her fingertips, cascading like water through a stream. The corner of the graveyard burned brightly in the light of the Will O' the Wisp. When the fire flickered away, all that remained was a large, black dog resembling a massive hound with thick fur and a bushy tail. It growled, baring its teeth as a ghostly chain swirled around it effortlessly.

"Oh man, a Barghest!" Percy exclaimed in fear.

"What the hell is that?" Lance asked, keeping his eyes on the creature.

"They're known by many names—Barghest, Grim, Black Shuck, and others. Normally, they protect cemeteries from graverobbers, but this one's different. They're usually not this aggressive. I think it's been enchanted."

Gwen heard Percy say that, and she knew exactly what that meant. *Morgan . . . That witch set a trap for us.* "So, how do we stop it?" she asked her gnome companion.

Percy shrugged bluntly. "I don't know. I've never had to fight one before. They usually only attack graverobbers, not humans or Fae wandering through the cemetery."

Gwen flexed her hand, staring at it before looking at the Barghest. "Well, if Morgan wants to see what I can do with this, let me show her!" She abruptly charged toward the Grim, surprising both Lance and Percy. The black dog attacked, sending the magical chain spinning toward her. Gwen knocked it away before using a gravestone to launch herself at the Barghest. With one punch from her armored fist, the Fae disappeared in a puff of black smoke.

Gwen huffed as she tried to catch her breath. She didn't realize that using the Pendragon put a strain on her spiritually and physically. Impressed with her performance, her friends gave her a thumbs-up and a round of applause. However, the Barghest was merely a distraction as Otis leaped out of the shadows and attacked Gwen.

"Look out!" Percy yelled, but it was too late. The ogre slammed his massive fist at her. Instinctively, she raised her hand to defend herself. Usually, the beast would splinter wood with a single blow, but all you heard was a loud clang of flesh on metal. Otis fell backward, screaming in pain as he grabbed his hand from the impact on the shield that appeared over Gwen's hand.

Her armored hand gripped a small golden shield. It shimmered in the dim light, decorated with a blue field with three golden crowns—the coat of arms of King Arthur Pendragon. She felt a surge of power flowing through her.

"Oh, radical!" Gwen said, surprised at the shield's sudden appearance. "This is just what I needed!"

Cecilia flew at the Pendragon from the treetops, extending her razor-sharp claws. Instinctively, Gwen bashed the shield into the harpy, knocking her away. She went flying toward Titus as he desperately attempted to save her from harm. Gwen stepped back, positioning herself between friend and foe.

"Well, well, well . . . It looks like you know how to use that power better than we expected," Maude said as she stepped out from the shadows with Prunella. Titus helped Otis up after he ensured Cecilia was okay. The entire gang moved in for the kill. "Unless you want something bad to happen to your friends, I suggest you surrender now, Gwen Iver."

"To who, you? Where's Morgan? I know she's the one behind this. If she wants the Pendragon, she can face me herself!"

"No, no, it doesn't work that way, Iver," Maude interrupted. "Morgan doesn't get her hands dirty with people like you. Now, either you surrender or your little friends suffer. The choice is yours."

Gwen did not know what to do, but before she could say anything, Percy stepped in front of her, fists clenched in defiance of the Dreadmoor Gang. "You leave Gwen alone!" he shouted. "You have no right to make demands of My Lady of the Pendragon!"

Maude and the rest of the gang reeled back in laughter at the audacity of the little gnome threatening them. Without thinking, Maude backhanded Percy across the face, sending the gnome flying backward into Gwen and Lance. The two immediately went to his aid and helped him up.

"Back off, you little freak. You know better than to talk to us that way," Maude said, but Percy grinned as he wiped his hand across his bloody lip.

"And you know better than to lay a hand on a Fae, little human," he reminded her. Suddenly, the ground shook violently as several stone figures—tiny at first but growing to more than seven feet tall—seemingly stepped out of the stone walls, rocks on the ground, and the gravestones. They were gangly with grotesque, misshapen heads. These were the Spriggans, the security force of the Fae. Typically, these monsters tormented and attacked humans in retaliation for any indiscretion toward the Fae. In Camelot Cove, they answered "only" to the Pendragon.

The Spriggans surrounded the Dreadmoor Gang. They stood in fear of the creatures, as the gang knew better than to try to fight them. The tallest of the monsters looked down at Maude as she stared at it. Her legs trembled with dread.

"Human, you dare lay a finger on this gnome!" the Spriggan leader shouted, his voice echoing off the stones, creating a constant reverberation. "Your punishment should be death, but I will leave that decision to the Pendragon."

The Spriggan turned toward Gwen and bowed. "My name is Hawthorn, my lady, leader of the Spriggans. What is your command? What shall we do with these troublemakers?" Gwen didn't realize how much power she had as the Pendragon, and she started to enjoy it more and more. She dismissed her armor and shield before she spoke to the Spriggan leader.

"First, I want to know where Artie Moor is. Prunella injected him with her venom, and I want to know he's safe."

Hawthorn turned to Prunella and scowled, causing her to turn away from his gaze. "You dare to bare your fangs on a human, Lamia? Where is this Artie Moor?" Prunella casually pointed toward a large willow tree off to the side. Lance and Percy rushed over and found Artie tied up, his eyes still glazed over from the venom's effects.

"He's okay, Gwen, but he's still under," Lance said as they freed him. That news satisfied Gwen but not Hawthorn. He snarled at the Dreadmoor Gang.

"Your actions walk a fine line, straddling the laws of the Fae," Hawthorn said to the Dreadmoor Gang's Fae members. "I will report your aggressive behavior to the elders of your clans, but be warned: any further action on your part will result in severe punishment. As for you, human girl, your fate is in the hands of the Pendragon."

Maude grimaced with a look of disgust at Gwen. However, this was something the Pendragon reveled in. She walked up to Maude and glared at her as a smirk crossed her lips. She usually would not do this, but Maude brought it on herself when she helped Morgan drug Artie and then smacked Percy the way she did.

"I'm going to let you off with a warning this time, Maude," Gwen said, knowing it would irritate her rival even more with her newfound cocky attitude. "But understand this—and let Morgan know too—if you come after my friends again to get to me, I will let the Spriggans enact their harshest punishment on you . . . all of you!"

With that, Gwen turned her back on them, adding insult to injury, before standing with her friends. "Let's go," Maude said, motioning to the others with a nod as the Spriggans opened their ranks to let the Dreadmoor Gang pass. Gwen could not help but notice the blood dripping from her clenched fists. Maude clenched them so tight that she cut into them with her nails, probably wanting to beat Gwen senseless. Fortunately, with the Spriggans around, she knew better. With scowls and some trepidation, the gang left the cemetery as fast as they could. Hawthorn smiled, or what could be construed as a smile on his rocky façade.

"You are wise beyond your years, Gwen Iver," he complimented, noting Gwen's remarkable insight. "You have a keen foresight in keeping the peace between humans and Fae. I see a lot of your mother and grandmother in you."

Upon hearing that, Gwen took another step closer to accepting the power of the Pendragon.

# Chapter Seven:

## *The Knights of the Pendragon*

Artie sat in Merle's kitchen and rubbed his forehead, trying to focus past the fog in his head. The venom from the Lamia still ran through his veins, and according to Uncle Merle, there was no antidote for it. All one could do was let it run its course while sipping ginger clove tea to soothe the effects.

"Drink up, boy, if you want to feel better," Merle advised while pouring tea for the others. Gwen sat beside Artie, rubbing his shoulder as she tried to ease his torment.

"Sorry, Merle, but tea isn't what I need," Artie countered. "I need a sledgehammer to take my sister apart, bit by bit, as she did to my head."

"I doubt that would work on her unless it were a magical sledgehammer," Lance joked. "You don't happen to have one with that armor, Gwen, like your shield?"

"This is not a joke, Lance du Lok. These attacks are quite brazen, especially for someone as cold and calculating as Morgan Moor."

"I doubt Morgan planned for things to happen that way. More than likely, Maude decided to do things independently," Gwen interjected. "Speaking of which, Uncle Merle, why does Maude Reddy have a beef with me? In all the years I've known her, we've never gotten along, but recently, this hatred has been on another level." Before he could answer, Triss and G Wayne barged in on the ensemble. Triss ran over and wrapped her arms around Gwen.

"Are you okay, Gwen? We heard through the Spriggan network about everything that happened in the cemetery!" Triss said, grasping Gwen's face with her hands, squeezing it between them. Lance and Artie appeared shocked and slightly surprised that their friends were elves.

"Woah, Triss, you're an elf?" Lance exclaimed.

"You too, G Wayne? What's going on?" Artie blurted out.

"What? Can you see us? How the Hell is that possible?" Triss asked.

"Artie got his fairy sight from Morgan, and I gave it to Lance, okay?" Gwen explained, causing the friends to ramble on, revealing their secrets and surprises, until Merle slammed his fist into the table.

"Can we please stop with the Human-Fae Mutual Appreciation Society? We have more important things to worry about," Merle shouted, causing everyone to be quiet. Once they all calmed down, he addressed Gwen.

"To answer your question, yearling, there's something you don't know about Maude Reddy. She's your cousin." That announcement was news to everyone there, including the Fae. It was a secret no one knew about except Merle and Viv.

"Your mother and her mother were sisters," Merle began. "But being the oldest, your mother was destined to inherit the Pendragon. When your parents died, Maude's mother was given a chance to assume the mantle, but she could not open the box. The Pendragon did not deem her worthy of the power. Distraught by her failure, she left Camelot Cove, never to be heard from again."

"So, in other words, Maude blames me for her mother abandoning her and that she should have inherited the power of the Pendragon, not me. Is that about right?" Gwen assumed. Merle pointed at her, affirming her deductions. Without warning, Gwen slammed her fist down on the table, startling everyone, but at least she didn't break the table. "And when would you tell me this little secret, Uncle Merle? Before or after she tried to kill me?"

"Gwen, don't be overly dramatic. I didn't tell you about Maude because Morgan Moor got to her first and pulled her into that little Dreadmoor Gang. Maude was a lost soul, and telling you about your connection to her made no sense."

"That's exactly why you should have told me," Gwen interrupted, jumping to her feet and leaning across the table toward him. "She's my cousin, so maybe there's a chance of getting her away from Morgan. Haven't you learned anything about humans in your immortal life, Merlin? Being lost doesn't mean you'll wander forever. It means you're waiting for someone to find you."

Merle listened to Gwen's rant, realizing his mistake in keeping the truth from her. "You're right, yearling. I should have told you about Maude. After your mother's death, I was so focused on keeping you safe that I was blinded to the other possibilities."

"So, what to do now, Uncle Merle?" Gwen said as she sat back down at the table, crossing her arms and glaring at him.

Merle sighed before he answered her. "The best thing you can do is wait for Morgan to make her move. This incident with the Spriggans will set back her plans for the time being. In the meantime, I suggest you find a way to fight back against her Dreadmoor Gang."

"And just how am I supposed to do that?" Gwen questioned rather sternly. "With all their muscle, it would be like hitting a brick wall with a twig."

"There you go again, always thinking with your fists instead of your head," Merle snapped at her, trying to put his ward in her place. "The first thing you need is allies. In the old days, the Pendragon gathered those loyal to her to fight against anyone who sought to corrupt the magic."

"You mean like the Knights of the Round Table, right Merlin . . . I mean, Uncle Merle," Artie said, immediately correcting himself as Merle glared at him for speaking out.

"Yes, Artie, but not as vivid as all that. You five should do nicely as Gwen's Knights of the Pendragon."

Gwen looked around at her friends, who seemed excited at the thought of helping her in her role as the Pendragon.

"What? Are you kidding me? I won't involve my friends in this and potentially get them hurt, maimed, or worse. No way!"

"Gwen, we want to help. It would be best if you didn't have to do this alone," Lance interjected. Everyone agreed with him wholeheartedly. These humans and Fae were eager to jump into the fray, but Gwen was having none of it.

"No!" she shouted, jumping to her feet. "No! I won't endanger my friends for your crazy crusade against some evil sorceress. I'm not doing it!" Gwen pushed her way past everyone and stormed out of the room.

Her friends tried to follow her, but Merle stopped them. "Let her go," he said as they stopped suddenly. "Gwen needs to figure this out for herself if she is to accept the power. Any doubt in her mind will cause her to falter, and the Pendragon will return to the box, awaiting the next descendant to take up the mantle."

"All the more reason we should go after her, old man," Triss yelled at Merle, taking him aback by her utter disrespect. "*Abota hanya ce da yawa ke tafiya amma kaɗan ne ke bi!*" She quoted an elf proverb, "Friendship is a road many travel but few tread."

"Gwen was right . . . After thousands of years, you still don't understand humans," Triss continued. "Growing up with someone like Gwen—her kind heart, overwhelming courage, and bright mind—taught me more about humanity in these few years than you learned in an immortal lifetime."

Triss leaned across the table, glaring at Merle. "If we don't show her our resolve to help her, she'll never accept the Pendragon. Gwen won't face this alone if WE have anything to say about it."

The rest of them agreed with Triss's comments and chased after Gwen. Merle sat quietly, sipping his tea, as a sly smile came across his face. *Young people are so predictable. All they need is the right push to motivate them.* Merle chuckled, knowing he had more insight into the human mind than these children realized.

Gwen rode hard and fast down the hill, away from the lighthouse, her uncle, and her friends. She was tired and confused about the whole situation. The last thing she wanted to do was put them all in danger from the likes of Morgan Moor. She did not stop, pushing herself to ride past the harbor and the boardwalk toward the outskirts of town. Ignoring the courteous hellos and well-wishes from people, Gwen feverishly rode her bike until she finally gave up and stopped to catch her breath.

*What do I do? I can't ask my friends to risk their lives for me and this stupid power.* Gwen's mind buzzed with frustration and insecurity. *I can't ask them to stand up to a killer like Morgan. I don't want to lose my friends like I lost my parents.* Suddenly, she heard a church bell ring and realized where she was. Her hard ride had taken her to St. Nicholas' Cathedral, the largest church in Camelot Cove. The teenager did not know what brought her there—maybe providence or coincidence. Either way, she needed a breather to find answers.

Gwen quickly parked her bike, went up the granite steps, and into the Gothic structure through the massive wooden doors. She had been baptized here, and although she did not remember the occasion, she had seen the pictures. Gwen was one of those occasional churchgoers—weddings, funerals, holidays, or special events.

She looked at the intricate archways and stained glass as she walked down the aisle and reflected on her faith. She believed in a higher power but always wondered why God let her parents die—no, murdered. Now her faith was being tested again with this entire situation.

Gwen sat down in a pew and quietly began to pray. She did not know what to say or ask. She only wanted a chance to clear her mind. She sobbed quietly, laying her head on her hands until a gentle hand touched her shoulder.

"Gwen, is everything all right?" Father Klaus Lindell asked. His dark hair, boyish looks, and clear plastic spectacles displayed a young age for a parish priest. He was new to St. Nicholas, so Gwen did not know much about him, but she had heard he was outgoing and kind. She slid over as he sat down next to her in the pew. He reached into his pocket and gave her his handkerchief to wipe the tears from her eyes and to blow her nose.

"Thank you," Gwen said as she tended to her emotions.

"I don't see you in here too often, so it's a surprise to find you all alone and crying. Is there anything I can help you with?" His soft-spoken voice eased the tension inside Gwen, but she knew he would not understand her problems.

"No, Father Klaus. I don't think you can," she said, wiping her eyes again. "It's difficult to explain what I'm going through right now."

"Well, taking on the mantle of the Pendragon is a lot for a fifteen-year-old girl. I expect that burden would weigh down on anyone's heart and soul." His revelation caught Gwen by surprise. She was amazed he knew about the Pendragon and the Fae.

"You . . . You know?"

"Well, of course, I do; all the priests and nuns in this parish know about you and the Fae," Father Klaus explained. "Clergy and nuns may only get assigned to Camelot Cove if they have a degree in ancient history and mythology."

"But doesn't the church view creatures of magic like the Fae as evil abominations or something like that?"

"No, of course not. Why would we?" he snapped back rather sternly. "All are God's creations, in Heaven and Earth, whether human or Fae. It's what you do with that power that determines your fate before the eyes of the Lord."

"Excuse me, Father Klaus," a shy voice interrupted them. Gwen looked up to see Mrs. Stonehaven, the church caretaker, standing in the aisle. She wore a flowing blue and white dress, and a pale lavender bonnet covered her head. Her silver hair was tied up neatly under the bonnet. Although her hair showed her age, her face did not, as it still looked young and vibrant. "Your dinner is getting cold, Father. Shall I keep it warm while you speak to Miss Iver, or will she join you for dinner?"

"Please keep it warm for me, Mrs. Stonehaven. I won't be too much longer." The woman gave a polite bow before turning to leave. As she walked away, her feet never touched the floor; she hovered just above it. Gwen realized that Mrs. Stonehaven was not human at all but a Fae.

"Mrs. Stonehaven is a Silkie, a spirit that inhabits homes to keep them clean and tidy. She has been with us since the church was built over five hundred years ago. Mrs. Stonehaven can be very temperamental. She does not tolerate laziness or tardiness very well and keeps us humans on our toes. We all have standards to maintain."

"That's incredible," Gwen muttered before she realized that her predicament still hung over her. "But to be honest, Father, that's my problem. I don't know if I'm up to the standards of being the Pendragon. Two days ago, I was an ordinary girl starting high school. Now, I'm supposed to be some savior of Camelot Cove."

"You're not a savior, Gwen Iver. There is only one savior in this world. You are a simple girl with an incredible gift—

a gift to help bridge the gap between humans and Fae. Lord only knows I've tried with little to no success."

"You, Father? How?" Gwen curiously inquired.

"Some of the Fae have come to accept God and even attend services here, but others believe in the edict of King Oberon and Queen Titania, the rulers of *Tír na nÓg.*"

"Who are they?"

"They are the rulers of the Fae," Father Klaus explained. "They live in the fairy kingdom of *Tír na nÓg.* They don't like the church or our presence in Camelot Cove. They have repeatedly called out the 'conquering God' as a misguided influence on the Fae as they attempt to sway them back to their side, but I digress. This is not about them. This is about you."

Father Klaus stood up from the pew and moved into the aisle. "You have a wonderful opportunity to help this community of humans and Fae continue to thrive, and yes, there are those who would seek to steal the Pendragon and corrupt our world. It's one of the reasons I'm here."

"What do you mean, Father?"

"The church believes that should the Armageddon come, it will begin here in Camelot Cove," he continued. "They see the power of the Pendragon as divine intervention in keeping the apocalypse at bay. Unlike your Uncle Merle and Lady Viviane, my job is to observe and interact but not intervene."

"What do you mean? Viv told me they only keep things from spreading beyond Camelot Cove into the human world?"

"That's partially true, but they also intervene between *Tír na nÓg* and human observers like myself."

"And what have you observed about me, Father Klaus?" Gwen asked, point blank. "What makes me worthy of being the Pendragon?" The priest leaned in close to answering her.

"I see a promising young woman with a good heart and friends willing to go to the ends of the Earth to protect her and their home." Father Klaus motioned toward the back of the church with a simple head nod. Gwen spun around to see all her friends waiting for her. They followed her to show her the love and support she desperately needed.

Gwen jumped out of the pew and ran to them, grabbing each in a group hug. She felt all her worries slip away when she realized she didn't need to make a decision—it was already made for her.

Father Klaus motioned the sign of the cross to bless them before walking away toward the rectory and his dinner. Mrs. Stonehaven did not like to be kept waiting.

Morgan slapped Maude across the face. For years, she became accustomed at dishing out constant abuse on her protege, knowing full well that the sting would linger for some time.

"How can you be so stupid?" Morgan screamed as she walked down the line of the Dreadmoor Gang, standing in attention resembling a military formation. "I told you to test her so I could observe her abilities and potential, not try to force her to surrender right then and there! These things take time and must be handled delicately, not rushed through like a bull in a China shop . . ." Morgan looked at

Titus after she made that comment, causing the minotaur to flinch slightly. "No offense, Titus."

"None taken," he gruffed back, huffing through his nostrils.

"And you know better than to slap around a Fae," she continued, storming over to Maude. "Now the Spriggans are involved, and those interfering grubs cannot be swayed or coerced to look the other way."

"I'm sorry, Morgan, but I thought that since she hadn't fully taken in the power of the Pendragon, as you said, it would be easy to take her down," Maude retorted, earning her a flick of Morgan's properly manicured finger on her forehead.

"What have I told you before? Don't think! I do all the thinking for you. Got it?" Morgan shouted. Maude could only nod quietly and obey her leader.

"So, what do we do now?" Maude asked meekly. Before she could answer, Sheriff Ulysses Moor rushed into the house. He huffed under the strain of his fat belly, which hung slightly over his belt. His uniform was neatly pressed, and he wore a wide-brimmed hat garnished with a star, denoting his authority.

"Sorry I'm late, Morgan honey, but it took a little longer to get a full answer from the Spriggans," he gasped, seemingly reporting to his daughter. "They don't hold you responsible for any of this, but they are aware of your connection to the Dreadmoor Gang and intend to keep a close eye on things for the time being."

Morgan fumed at the news as she pleaded with her father to try and sway him. "Daddy, can't you make them stop? I was nowhere near the cemetery when all this happened. It was a simple misunderstanding, and you know that?"

"I do, pumpkin, I do. Your stepbrother got you into this mess, and I will punish Artie severely when he gets home," Sheriff Moor dictated. "But for the time being, I suggest you back off from Gwen Iver. Now that she's become the Pendragon, there is much more scrutiny from the entire Fae community. I can't protect you from all of them."

Morgan bit down on her knuckle, a nervous tick of hers when things did not go her way. She relented to her father's wishes and would bide her time. "Okay, Daddy, I'll do as you say, but leave poor Artie alone. I don't want to cause any undue friction with the little princess. However, there is something I need you to do for me."

"Anything, Morgan. What is it you need?"

Morgan was thrilled at how easily she manipulated and controlled her father. Getting him to kill her stepmother and make it look like an accident was simple. She could not have another woman competing for her father's love or power in the house. Right now, what she needed was his hobby.

"Daddy, could you use your darling woodworking skills to make me a puzzle box?" she asked with a sly smile. Morgan bided her time, but before the winter break, she would force Gwen Iver to surrender the Pendragon.

# Chapter Eight:

## *On the Wings of a Dragon*

Gwen flew backward and slammed hard into the ground. She rubbed her bottom, sore from hitting the floor for the third time. This time, it was because of a lightning bolt from Merlin's staff. This was another disappointing conclusion to her weekly training in the grotto.

"Come on, yearling, on your feet," Merlin said, tapping his staff on the stone floor. This outcropping overlooking the water was usually a place for meditation and contemplation. Merlin decided it would be the best place to train Gwen. Down by the roaring waters of the lake, in the presence of the Pendragon, Gwen could feel the flow of magic directly from the source.

Gwen slowly returned to her feet, chaffing at his "yearling" remark. Whether Merle or Merlin, she hated being called that nickname. "I don't get it," Gwen remarked with a hint of frustration. "I destroyed a Barghest and stopped an ogre's fist. Why can't I stop your magic?"

"Well, in the first place, I am far more powerful than a Barghest or an ogre," Merlin boasted. "And secondly, you are doing it to yourself, Gwen. You are barely accessing the power of the Pendragon. You will never hold your own in a fight by summoning only the armor and shield."

"I am sick and tired of you always talking to me in riddles!" Gwen screamed. "I don't understand what you need me to do! I am a teenager from northern Michigan, not some sorcerer's apprentice in a magic castle!"

Gwen aimed her rage directly at Merlin. The old wizard sighed loudly, adding to her frustration. "I am sorry if my training regime is difficult for you, but I'm not used to this either. The Pendragon normally trained their heir for thousands of years, but now it's just me and you, Gwen." His advice fell on deaf ears as the emotional teenager had none of it.

"Listen to me, yearling . . ."

"Stop calling me that!" Gwen shouted in anger. "I hate it when you call me that! Why do you constantly call me that name?"

Merlin paused, gritting his teeth before he answered her. "Because it's what your father called you," he said. Gwen stepped back and collapsed on the bottom step, shocked and unnerved at Merlin's words. The old wizard took a deep breath and sat on the stairs beside her. Gwen was still reeling from what Merlin said as she tried to comprehend how she should feel.

"On the day you were born, your father was rushing home. You were not born in a hospital but here in Camelot

Cove," Merlin explained. "Because of the Fae, we use midwives to care for the birth of our children, but especially for the Pendragon."

"Really? Why?"

"Well, birth can be quite an emotional experience, and since the power reacts to emotion, it can run amok inside a pregnant woman whose hormones are out of control." Merlin could see Gwen did not fully understand his explanation, and he turned red from embarrassment as he thought of ways to explain it better. "I suggest you talk to Viv and have her explain it to you, okay?"

Gwen nodded, not wanting to embarrass him any further. "Anyway, he nearly hit a deer and her little fawn in his rush to get home. He saw it as a providence of fate with your birth. From that moment on, he started calling you 'yearling' when he held you in his arms."

Gwen started to cry. She had never heard this before, like the many things she was told and experienced over the past month. Merlin reached over and took her by the hand to comfort her emotional turmoil.

"Your father was one of the bravest men I have ever known. I started calling you yearling out of respect for him," Merlin continued. "He married your mother knowing that his life and the lives of his children could be threatened. He didn't care. He loved your mother and wanted to protect her at all costs. After you were born, he was even more determined to be there for both of you."

Gwen wiped the tears from her eyes as she got back on her feet and stepped back into position to continue her training. Merlin took the hint and moved across from her. "Merlin, can you tell me more about my mom and dad? I don't mean the loving parent stuff you told me over the years, but more like what you just told me."

"Of course I will, Gwen," he replied with a sly smile.

"You know, you can call me yearling whenever you like," Gwen answered, bringing them a little closer in their relationship. "Please tell me how I'm supposed to use this power properly."

"All right. Think back to when you fought in the cemetery. When you reached under the hood of the Will O' the Wisp and touched the magic, what did that feel like?"

Gwen thought momentarily, remembering the warmth that tickled her from her fingers up her arm. "It was warm but not like reaching into an open flame. It was like wrapping up in a blanket on a cold winter night."

"And when you fought the Barghest and the ogre—what were you thinking about when you struck back at them?"

"I was worried about Artie. I wanted to do whatever I could to save him."

"That's exactly what you need to control the power of the Pendragon," Merlin explained. "Every time you summon this power, you will use it to protect the people of Camelot Cove—both human and Fae. Using that conviction to control the magic directed at you would be ideal. Let it wrap around you like that warm blanket you so fondly recall. That is how you use this power."

Gwen understood what he was telling her as she raised her shield to defend herself from his attack, bracing herself by digging the soles of her feet into the ground. Merlin tapped his staff once on the ground as thunder could be heard outside. A lightning bolt lanced into the grotto from one of the openings in the sea wall, bouncing off his staff and toward Gwen.

She felt the impact off her shield, but this time was different. Gwen let it travel up her arm through the armor, tingling as it flowed around her. She thought about the static electrical charge one gets rubbing their feet on a carpet and touching a doorknob. Then, in one swift motion, Gwen swung her shield, flinging the lightning bolt away.

It was the first time she had done that in her training with Merlin. Gwen felt proud of herself, finally finding the key to controlling her newfound power. As happy as he was for her, Merlin could see Gwen getting a little cocky. "It was one time, yearling. Save your party for after you've done that a hundred times," he said, "but that's enough for today. I think it's best to discover your connection to the Pendragon directly from the source."

"The source? What do you mean?" Gwen asked, but a rumbling echoed through the cavern before he could answer. The majestic golden dragon rose from the water below and stared at Gwen before it lowered its head to the edge of the stone outcropping.

"Go ahead, hop on," Merlin said, surprising Gwen completely.

"What? On that? You want me to get on a dragon?"

"It's time you see Camelot Cove from a different perspective," Merlin said. "The Pendragon will take you around and reveal more than what simple fairy sight will. I think it will be an eye-opening experience for you."

"But won't people see me flying about on a giant golden dragon?" Gwen asked, worried about her already growing reputation as the Pendragon.

"Haven't you learned anything about magic yet, yearling? The Pendragon has lived here for thousands of years, and no one has discovered it outside our community. When we first arrived, the indigenous people helped us settle in. Then the Western expansion brought our

European family into the area—the French, Dutch, English, and even some Vikings too. They remembered the ancient myths and legends of the Fae, so these first human settlers became a part of our community. From that day on, Camelot Cove was born.

"The Pendragon has existed here and will continue to live here," he continued. "The humans and the Fae of our little community know it's here. The sword sitting on the rock is the proof of its existence."

"You mean the sword on Founder's Rock? That's real? I mean, is that what I think it is?"

"Yes, *Excalibur*, the King's Sword," Merlin added. "It has remained there as a symbol of the power of the Pendragon."

"So, why don't I have a weapon instead of this armor?"

"The Pendragon is the defender of Camelot Cove, not its ruler," Merlin explained. "You are not a warrior, yearling. Not yet, at least. Now, climb on the dragon."

Apprehension sunk in as Gwen looked at the dragon. She tried to figure out where to get on. Merlin chuckled under his breath. Gwen could not tell if he was laughing at her or the awkward situation. "Sit at the nape of the neck, Gwen. The dragon will ensure nothing happens to you."

Gwen had experienced so many strange things these past few weeks, so what was one more? She took a deep breath before climbing on. She grabbed onto two bony spikes from its neck and squeezed her legs to get a firm grip. Without warning, the dragon suddenly dived down into the water. The cold water chilled Gwen as she held her breath at the dunking. The dragon swam through an underwater tunnel before entering the lake and breaking through the water, soaring into the air.

Gwen coughed violently, expelling the water she swallowed. "You could have warned me!" she shouted, cursing at the dragon until she saw the landscape below her. The lake stretched out for miles in every direction. Her eyes followed the coastline of the Northern Peninsula of Michigan to the east and west and across the lake to the Canadian side. The moonlight danced across the water, glistening off the surface like a mirror. There were lights from many fishing boats, ferry boats, and pleasure craft traversing the great lake. From high above, Gwen saw the glow of her town, both the electric lights from the homes and businesses and the magical lights generated by the Fae. Gwen then realized she was soaring more than a mile into the night sky.

"Holy . . . I'm flying! I'm really flying! Woo-hoo!" Gwen screamed at the top of her lungs as she raised her arms, cheering loudly.

*Are you enjoying yourself, Gwen Iver?* A voice rang out in her head, one she had never heard before. It took a moment for Gwen to realize that the dragon was speaking to her.

"You can talk?" she asked curiously. "Why didn't you say anything in the cave?"

*The grotto suppresses the magic to keep me well-protected. Merlin and Lady Viviane only occasionally let me out to stretch my wings. It helps restore the flow of magic from the source to the Pendragon.*

"But I thought you were the Pendragon?"

*Yes and no. I am the source of the magic, while you are the receptacle.* The more she thought about it, the more the explanation made sense to Gwen.

"So, you're like a battery, and I guess that makes me the flashlight, right?" Gwen tried to articulate it as best she could, earning a slight nod from the golden dragon. "So, do you have a name?"

*None that you could pronounce with your human tongue, and please don't call me 'Goldie' like some of your predecessors did. I hate that blatantly obvious name.* Gwen thought for a minute before an idea came to her.

"What about Hugh, since you're such a beautiful golden luster?" Although it was hard to tell, Gwen could see a slight smile emerge on its face.

*That is the first original name given to me by a Pendragon. Thank you, Gwen Iver. Now, let me spread my wings and show you the true nature of our beautiful world.* Hugh flapped his wings and let out a roar that could be heard for miles. To the people below, it rumbled like thunder, but it was the sound of a dragon taking flight.

*Protect yourself with the Pendragon, Gwen Iver. Use the armor to draw power from me into you.*

Gwen placed her armored hand against the dragon's scales. She remembered the warmth and comfort of the flame when she felt the fire of the Will O' the Wisp. Reaching out, she drew that same power—the magic of the Pendragon—into her. Her armor glowed with a soft magical light, wrapping around her from her fingertips to her toes.

Before she realized it, Gwen was speeding through the atmosphere, crossing the Rocky Mountains as the snow wisped off the peaks and chilled the air. She felt nothing as the dragon picked up speed, reaching the deep blue waters of the Pacific Ocean in no time flat. She watched as whales migrated in packs through the waters off the coast of Oregon. Hugh continued west until they watched the sun rise over the shores of Japan. She saw the sights and sounds of this ancient country filled with modern technology begin their day anew.

Hugh quickly turned south until they reached the continent of Australia, passing over the red rock mountain of *Uluru* in the heart of the outback. It was strange, as Gwen felt a sense of magic in this place like she did in Japan when they passed over it.

"Hugh, is there magic here and in Japan?" Gwen asked.

*Of course. I do this flight to replenish the magic from the most sacred sites all around the world. Camelot Cove may be the heart of magic, but its arteries stretch across the planet.* Hugh continued his flight to various points—the pyramids of Egypt, the Black Forest in Germany, Stonehenge and Glastonbury Tor in Great Britain, the Azores, Intikancha in Peru, Easter Island, and more. Hugh followed the flow of the ley lines—the magic bands of energy that connected these magical sights worldwide—before returning to Camelot Cove.

*The ley lines intersect here in Camelot Cove. It's one of the reasons Merlin chose to make this place our home.* Hugh made one final pass over the city as Gwen caught her breath from her magical experience. She saw more of the world in one night than she could ever imagine.

"Thank you, Hugh. You've opened my eyes to what it means to be the Pendragon." As Hugh turned to head back to the lighthouse, Gwen saw something out of the corner of her eye. She spotted Maude Reddy's home. She lived in an apartment over the post office with her father. She saw that a light was still on in her bedroom, and her curiosity got the best of her.

"Hugh, no one can see us, right? Not human or Fae?" Gwen asked.

*Yes, Gwen Iver, but why do you ask?*

"Can you do me a favor? I want to see something," Gwen asked, explaining what she wanted. The dragon listened to her request and swooped down, landing next to the post office. It stretched up so Gwen could peer into Maude's room. She knew it might be wrong, probably illegal, but she wanted to learn more about her cousin beyond the deep-seated hatred and rivalry.

She watched as Maude played on an elaborate gaming computer console. She played Gwen's favorite online video game, *Space Legion*, and was terrific at it. It took her a moment to finally catch her handle from her heads-up display. Gwen even recognized the name. It was someone she had even teamed up with on missions and quests in the past. The two were hated rivals, and yet they found commonality in the personas they played online.

*Maybe I can get her away from Morgan's clutches.* She thought about ways to reach Maude when she watched her attack the enemy lines in the game. "Die, princess, die!" she shouted into her headset as she bashed in the enemy Dragknight forces.

*Then again, maybe not.*

Gwen strolled through the high school library, her fingers gently running across the binding of each one as she carefully read the titles. She wanted to learn more about the Fae and the many places of magic she visited on Hugh. Gwen thought that the more she understood these people and places, the better it would help her integrate with the Pendragon.

She shook her head in frustration, unable to find what she searched for. There were basic books on mythology, but nothing more substantial or in-depth. Artie warned her that the school library had slim pickings, and he would know.

"Is there something, in particular, you're looking for, Miss Iver?" Mrs. Layla Khalil approached Gwen, eager to help with her query. Her appearance initially startled Gwen, but it made perfect sense for a librarian. Layla was a sphinx, a beautiful woman with the body of a lion, a serpent for a tail, and the wings of an eagle. She always wondered why the aisles were wider than most, and seeing the librarian in her proper form, Gwen understood why.

Even with her Fae form, Layla still dressed appropriately for school—a stylish blouse and colorful scarf with her reading glasses hanging on a chain around her neck. Her olive skin radiated the beauty of this ancient creature. The wisdom and knowledge associated with the sphinx made her a perfect educator for the children of Camelot Cove.

"Yes, Mrs. Khalil, I hoped to read up on the different Fae clans to help me understand them more. I thought there would be more information in the library."

"Well, normally, you would be right, but the Fae are quite particular about protecting our history. The books humans write about us are so outrageous and filled with lies that we don't allow them here. It would be too confusing to our younger generation."

Gwen chuckled at the misunderstanding between humans and Fae on a cultural level. "That's true. Humans have an overactive imagination regarding things we don't understand."

"Yes indeed. Why, when those *Twilight* books came out, I nearly had a riot on my hands between the vampires and the werewolves. It was madness." The women laughed at the reference before Layla had to shush them for being too loud in the library.

"Well, that makes sense. What about something on sacred sights related to magic? I think Hugh said something about ley lines."

"Hugh?" Gwen saw the confused look, something out of the ordinary for a sphinx. Triss told her that the librarian was a Fae with an eidetic memory and a hunger for new information.

"Sorry, it's the Pendragon. I call him Hugh. He took me on a flight around the world last night. We visited all these different places following the ley lines. I think he called them that."

"Amazing, I never knew the Pendragon did that. Do you think Merl . . . Would your Uncle Merle allow me to speak with the dragon? I would love to know more about its activities."

"I don't see why not, but you better let me ask him first. In the meantime, do you have something on ley lines?"

"Let me check our reference room. I might have something there that interests you." Layla left Gwen alone while she searched for the right book. Gwen continued to look through the stacks for anything else.

"My, aren't we the busy little bee, Gwen," Morgan said as she approached Gwen down the aisle. "Usually, I expect to find Artie buried in these books, not you. I see my little stepbrother rubbing off on you. Is there something I should know about you and Artie? Come on; you can tell me, woman to woman."

Morgan drew out the ire in Gwen, hoping for a confrontation to see what she was made of, but the Pendragon knew better than to get drawn into a fight in school. "Artie is my good friend, and he does rub off on me," Gwen shot back at her. "He told me that, in war, the best weapons can be found in the library."

"War? And who are you at war with, Gwen darling? The fishermen or the tourists?" Morgan laughed at her outrageous comment. "Or perhaps there's someone else that threatens you."

"Since my parents were killed mysteriously, I can't be sure if and when my life could be in danger. You have to be prepared to defend yourself, no matter who or what may threaten you, even snot-nosed bitches who consider themselves above reproach."

Morgan took her threat to heart and stepped into Gwen. She stood inches taller than the Pendragon, primarily due to the stiletto heels she wore. The two squared off, silent in their opposition to the other. Morgan had a slight smirk on her face while Gwen stood firm and stoic.

Morgan glanced at the stacks of books and reached up to pull a book down from the shelf before handing it to Gwen. "If you want to prepare yourself for war, Gwen Iver, I might recommend reading this book. If you want to know who your enemy truly is, you might find it a rather enlightening read."

Gwen snatched up the book as Morgan walked off, not saying another word. Gwen did not take her eyes off her until she left the library. Finally, she looked at the book title. "*Le Morte d'Arthur* . . . The Death of Arthur," she read, flipping through the pages until she saw something rather peculiar written in pencil in the margin. "*'Morganna Le Fay was a powerful female figure in the Arthurian legends. She represents control, sorcery, and manipulation. She used underhanded, often manipulative methods to create her power."*

Gwen looked again toward the library entrance, looking for Morgan, but she was already gone. As she reread the passage in the margins, Gwen noticed similar notes in the margins throughout the book. Something came over her as she read the various notes scattered through the pages. "I know this handwriting," she muttered before flipping to the end to read the card catalog entry. It was an old reference card previously used to check out books before computer bar codes modernized library collections.

A tear came to her eye when she saw the name of the last person to check out this book—Helena Leode. It was her mother. She made these notes while researching Camelot Cove in her duties as the Pendragon, just like Gwen did now.

"Thanks, Mom!" Gwen whispered as she closed the book, holding it close to her heart. Her mother was still with her, helping her through these challenging times. A warmth swept over her, like the magic flowing from Hugh through the armor. It was as if her mother reached out to help Gwen make that connection.

"Gwen, are you all right?" Layla asked as her gentle touch comforted the teenager. Gwen smiled and nodded, wiping away the tears before handing the school librarian the book Morgan gave her.

"I'll take this one too, Miss Khalil." Morgan made a terrible mistake. She thought she could scare Gwen into giving up the Pendragon, but thanks to her mother, she was more determined than ever to master the ancient power.

## Chapter Nine:

### *Blood is Thicker than Water*

Fall in Camelot Cove was filled with excitement and wonder, especially for Gwen and her friends. Over the past several weeks, they experienced their hometown in a new light. It was a memorable time with high school football games, harvest festivals and parades, pumpkin and apple picking, and the approach of Halloween. The crisp, cool air and the smell of burning leaves, apple cider, and cut hay filled their senses as autumn settled in.

Seeing the Fae in their natural form became a new learning experience, and this time of the year made it even more spectacular. For the Fae, All Hallows Eve was akin to the Christmas holiday for humans. It was their celebration of life, love, and family.

Streets, stores, and homes were decorated in the colors of autumn—red, yellow, orange, brown, and black—for the sacred Fae holiday. Candlelight danced in the windows as preparations were made, including great feasts, parties, and various cultural celebrations. The multiple races of the Fae always came together at Halloween, but they each had their distinct way of commemorating the occasion.

The elves danced under the full moon to celebrate the season as the stars twinkled in the autumn sky. Dwarves feasted and drank to their heart's content, spending hours reveling in the glories of their ancestors. It was the spawning season for mermen and mermaids, so their time was spent with their significant others. Centaurs and fauns raced through the woods and along the beaches, competing with each other in athletic competitions. Many shops and businesses closed early to allow everyone to join the celebrations.

Camelot Cove High School was no exception. The student council decked the school in Fall colors and assorted decorations for All Hallows Eve. The upcoming Halloween Dance was one of the school year's most significant events, bigger than even homecoming or prom. Through all the festivities, academics and athletics still took priority.

Gwen hated the new limelight shining on her. As the Pendragon, all the Fae and some humans knew about her coming into her own. At sixteen, if they were deemed reliable, most human children were told the truth about Camelot Cove and given the fairy sight. This revelation made Gwen much more popular in school than she wanted.

People she had known since elementary school treated her differently. While some strove to get closer to her and tried to garner favor, others suddenly shunned Gwen. Her presence meant closer scrutiny of their extracurricular activities. These were usually considered simple pranks, but anyone from their respective clans finding out usually meant serious trouble. Gwen's presence dampened their style, but they could do nothing to avoid her, especially during school hours.

For her part, Gwen gave in to the idea of being the Pendragon, but she was desperate to maintain the life of an average high school student. She participated in after-school activities and clubs and stuck diligently to her studies. She even tried out for the cheerleading squad, hoping to join and participate in something fun. She planned to keep the overarching responsibility of duty from dictating her day-to-day life in Camelot Cove.

Her friends kept their promise to support her every step of the way. Gwen was always escorted by one or more of them to and from school or whenever she was in town. During the school day, she was closely watched by teachers and administrators for her protection. The threat of Morgan and her Dreadmoor Gang remained a constant danger to the teenager.

The bell rang, echoing the ever-shifting class schedule, leaving ten minutes for students to rush from one class to the next. Geometry was not one of her favorite subjects, but Gwen knew she needed to improve on the poor performance on her last test. As the room slowly emptied, Gwen noticed Maude gathering her things together. Having the reputation of a dumb thug, she held her own pretty well in geometry, but Gwen was not interested in her math skills. She had been waiting more than a month to talk to Maude, and this might be the best chance to confront her about their linked heritage.

She waited until the last person left the room, leaving only the two behind. Maude did not even acknowledge her. She casually picked up her books and headed toward the door. "When were you going to tell me?" Gwen abruptly asked, stopping Maude in her tracks. "Were you ever going to tell me we're related?"

After a few moments of hesitation, Maude finally turned and looked at Gwen. Her lips twitched with anger. "Tell you what, cuz?"

"All these years we've known each other, you never once thought to tell me we're cousins. Why not?"

"Why don't you ask your guardian that question? I'm sure he had his reasons," Maude retorted, waving it off as she started to leave.

"Oh, trust me, Uncle Merle already got an earful for keeping this secret from me. That's the one thing I hate about this place—too many secrets. But I want to know why YOU didn't tell me. What did I ever do to you to make you hate me?"

"You need to ask me that?" Maude said, spinning around as she glared at Gwen. "You stole everything from me: my mother, my home, and the Pendragon itself. I have every reason in the world to hate you."

"I did none of those things!" Gwen shouted back at her, moving closer toward Maude. "I lost MY parents, MY home, and grew up in a lighthouse on a cliff. I didn't get this power until I opened that stupid box, and I still don't understand it completely. You should feel lucky that your mother didn't open the box. Otherwise, Morgan would have killed her like she did my parents."

"What are you talking about? Morgan was a child when your parents died. That was her birth mother or someone else who did that. She had nothing to do with their accident."

"Morgan Moor is Morgana le Fay, a sorceress who has lived for thousands of years, repeatedly reincarnating through history. That's her power. When she killed my mom and failed to take the Pendragon, she transferred her consciousness into a new body, into the Morgan Moor we know today. It's what she's done for centuries to try and possess the Pendragon."

Maude looked dumbfounded by what Gwen was saying. Since becoming the Pendragon, Gwen had learned much about Morgan Moor from the Fae. She was known for her knowledge of magic, history, the Fae, and more. Still, Gwen could see the doubt building in Maude's eyes. Maybe she had started to believe that her ramblings were possible.

"You're spouting nonsense," Maude countered. "You don't know a thing about Morgan or any of us in the Dreadmoor Gang."

"I know a lot more than you do," Gwen responded with affirmation and a sly grin. "Did you know Otis likes to draw manga? We share an art class, and he has an incredible talent. He loves the Japanese culture because they respect ogres, not fear them. The teacher always praises him for his work, although he won't show it to anyone else. He's very private about his art.

"Then there's Prunella. We're in home economics class together. She has an insatiable sweet tooth, so she loves to bake," Gwen continued, confusing Maude even more.

"Bake? You mean like cake and cookies?"

"Exactly. She seems to be trying to distance herself from her Lamia heritage through baked goods, and she's good, too. Her chocolate chip cookies are to die for."

"And Titus and Cecilia? What about them?" Maude asked.

"Those two are the 'Romeo and Juliet' of Camelot Cove," Gwen replied. "Their species of Fae normally despise each other, yet those two are head over heels in love. Their families don't like them being in a relationship, but they don't care. They prove that love transcends even magic."

Gwen could tell that Maude was impressed by her inability to come back at her. In over a month, she learned more about her friends than she probably knew herself. "So tell me, princess, what do you know about me?"

Gwen smiled wickedly; she was waiting for Maude to ask her that question. "Oh, I know a lot about you, 'Mordred_1188'—"

Maude interrupted. "What did you say? How do you know that name?"

"How could I not know the Stellar Centurion who beat the Divine Halo mission in *Space Legion* solo? Unlike you, I would have never attempted that frontal assault through the Reptilian Dragknight front lines. You barely had any health left, yet still managed to win."

"I didn't know you played *Space Legion: Final Frontier*. What's your handle?"

"GIDoll_1217," Gwen stated with a half-hearted salute. Maude's mouth dropped, shocked when she realized who Gwen was in the game.

"Wait, GI Doll? The best sniper in *Space Legion*? That's you? I mean, you saved my butt at Haldur's Pass," Maude said, seemingly excited for the first time since they started talking.

"Well, I needed you to get past the perimeter guards to get into the outpost to complete the mission. Besides, I didn't know it was you until you got in there and started shouting 'die princess die' to every Dragknight you fought against."

Gwen desperately tried to reach out to Maude through the one thing they had in common—online video games. Through the magic of the Pendragon, she felt an emotional surge from her cousin. *Maybe I am finally getting through to her?*

"So why aren't you online more often? You played most of the summer, but it dropped off when school started."

"Yeah, well, Uncle Merle has my gaming system in a lock box," Gwen explained. "I get the key to it when I bring home an A or a B. That C- I got on the last geometry quiz put me on lockdown. Speaking of which, how are you so good at geometry? I didn't expect you to be such a math whiz."

Maude laughed at being better than Gwen at something. "I make my money in the pool hall. Playing pool is all about the angles, so the better I calculate them, the more cash I can earn."

Gwen was starting to enjoy getting to know this side of Maude. In these few short moments, she learned more about her long-lost cousin than she did in the years she had known her. She was getting past all those defenses and recriminations Morgan placed on her. The smile on her face, something rare for Maude, let Gwen know she was reaching her.

"Look, Maude, I know you may not believe me about Morgan, but I gotta warn you. She's evil and will stop at nothing to get the Pendragon, even if it means destroying our town. I'm not trying to tell you what to do, but I know how she likes to take her aggressions out on the Dreadmoor

Gang, especially you." Gwen's admission struck a chord with

Maude as if she had discovered a secret.

"How do you know that?" Maude stammered.

"I see the bruises and cuts on you all the time. Your dad

is among the nicest people in town, so I know he's not

hurting you. Artie told me how Morgan treats you, and it's

not right." Gwen knew she had to speak up for Maude

without pushing her hard on the subject.

"Sorry, princess, but you know nothing about me or my

friends, especially Morgan. She's looked after me since I was

a kid. She may be a little hurtful sometimes, but that's only

because she looks out for number one, and so do I."

Gwen was afraid she may have taken things too far, but

she had to at least try and get through to Maude. "You're

right, Maude. I don't know as much about you as Morgan,

but I hope you'll give me a chance someday."

"Excuse me, ladies," Principal Cornelius interrupted,

startling the two of them. He stared at them intently from

the doorway over the top of his glasses. "You might want to

forgo this family reunion right now and get to your next class before I write you both up for tardiness."

The girls looked up at the clock and realized they were running late. The two clutched their books as they hurried out of the classroom, and students for the next class started to filter in, rushing past the principal. They glanced at each other, a mutual understanding that their conversation was not over. The long-lost cousins still had a lot to talk about.

The last bell rang, and the school day ended, sending hundreds of high school students running off campus to head home to an after-school job or their favorite hangout. As the students scattered, Maude hung back, leaning against the stone archway near the entrance to the school grounds. She watched as Gwen Iver rode off with Lance and Artie. Usually, she would seethe with rage at the sight of the little princess, but not today.

Her mind had been confused since her conversation with Gwen after geometry class. Maude admired that her cousin played the same online game she did and was good at it. Plus, what she said about Morgan made her question her true intentions. *Would Morgan have killed my mom or me to get her hands on the Pendragon? Is she that ruthless?* Every question led to another, then another, as her muddled thoughts grew.

"Hey, Maude," a voice cried out, breaking Maude out of her funk. She spied Prunella slithering toward her. She carried a small cardboard box delicately in her hands. "Morgan wants to see us at The Docks after school."

The Docks was a local hangout near the waterfront for most school kids. It was designed after an old-fashioned soda shop, serving burgers, fries, ice cream, and shakes. Maude knew that if Morgan wanted to meet at The Docks, she had her plan to take the Pendragon ready to go.

"Yeah, okay, Prunella. Thanks." Maude pulled a toothpick from her vest pocket and stuck it in her mouth. It was a bad habit, but to Maude, it helped her concentrate. As she chewed on the toothpick, she noticed the box Prunella was carrying.

"What's in the box?" Maude asked curiously.

"Oh, we made Halloween macarons in 'Home Ec' today. I thought Morgan might like them. Mrs. Frisbee said I was a talented baker and recommended me for a part-time job as an apprentice at Peter's Bake Shop. I hope that by giving these to Morgan, I could ask to take time away from the gang to work at the bakery. It would be a dream come true for me."

Maude remembered what Gwen had mentioned about Prunella's baking skills. Strangely, she never knew this about someone she always hung out with. "Morgan hates sweets. She says they cause her to break out in zits," Maude explained. "I would wait until she gets the Pendragon to ask her for permission."

"Oh, okay," Prunella said meekly. Maude could see that she was disheartened having her dreams set aside, and she hated being the one who hurt Prunella. This was a new sensation for her, and Maude wanted to rectify the situation as best as possible.

"Could I try one of your cookies?" she asked.

"They're not cookies. They're macarons—it's French. But sure, you can try one," Prunella said, opening the box. Inside were pumpkin orange macarons filled with white buttercream frosting. "It has a cream cheese frosting with pumpkin butter in the middle." Maude reached in and took one, pulling the toothpick out of her mouth before taking a bite—the sweet taste of the frosting with the tart pumpkin butter made for a delicious macaron.

"Wow, Prunella, that's delicious!" Maude complimented.

"You think so? Thanks!" Prunella said with a bright smile. Maude reached for another one before the two started heading toward The Docks.

"I heard you make a great chocolate chip cookie. I'd love to try them sometime," Maude said as she devoured the macarons.

"Sure, I'd be happy to bake some for you. The secret is the pinch of nutmeg I put in them. It brings out the chocolate flavor." The two talked more about baking and other things as they got to know each other better over a box

of sweet treats.

# Chapter Ten:

## *The Secret of Morgan Moor*

The Docks was a bustling whirlwind of excitement, music, fun, and food. Situated at the end of the boardwalk overlooking the cove, The Docks were two floors of entertainment. It was designed to bring the children—humans and Fae—together as cultures collided and intermingled in this popular establishment. Some human children knew about their Fae counterparts, while others were oblivious, but they all came together to let loose and have a good time.

Like any group of teenagers, certain "cliques" stayed together even though most of them mixed and mingled. The goblins, boggarts, and gorgons kept to themselves in a dark corner of the room, where only a few human wannabes dared to venture on the dark side. They were not troublemakers but rather mischief-makers who walked a fine line.

Across the way, some dryads, naiads, and sylphs hung around one table while young men vied for the attention of these captivating beauties. They had their pick of suitors but mostly ignored their unwanted advances. These Fae were more caught up in themselves and the latest fashion and beauty trends than hooking up with someone.

There was always a new competitor for The Docks' famous "Sword in the Stone" burger challenge. A towering pile of meat and cheese rested on a mountain of French fries in front of a human, a faun, and a changeling at the restaurant counter. Surrounded by assorted people and Fae to cheer them on, the three tried to eat the enormous pile of food in under fifteen minutes.

Besides the cliques and food challenges, most of The Docks was filled with couples sparking romance and friends discussing the latest video games. With all the strange and unusual beings filling every corner of the hangout, it was the place to be for students in Camelot Cove, but there was one area that was "by invitation" only.

Morgan worked her charms on the owner to get a private room at The Docks for her to conduct business and relax. On the third floor, what used to be a secondary storeroom was now a private room for the Dreadmoor Gang to use as they pleased. This room was their hangout with comfortable furniture, a private kitchen for food and drink, a pool table, and other gaming fun.

Maude challenged Titus at the pool table as Prunella and Cecilia watched the game from the sofa while enjoying what was left of Prunella's delicious macarons. It was not much of a match as Maude kept a steady pace of sinking shots. On the other hand, Otis sat alone across the room at a table. He focused diligently on his artwork. His tongue stuck out from the side of his mouth, and he squinted his eyes, staring as he carefully dragged his pencil across the paper.

"So, where's Morgan? I thought she called this meeting?" Titus asked while he waited for Maude to make her shot. His poor attempt to distract her from sinking the next shot was all for naught. Maude quickly made the ball bank off the rail and dropped it into the side pocket.

"Morgan went to get her nails done. She'll be here when she gets here," Maude said as she moved around the billiard table to set up her next shot.

"Wow, Prune, these are delicious!" Cecilia cooed over her macarons. "Can you make some for my mom to try? But they would need to be dairy and egg-free. My mom's gone vegan on me; some big health kick. It's gross."

"I have to ask Mrs. Frisbee how to do that, but I could try," Prunella replied, seemingly overjoyed that her friends liked her baking.

"Yeah, I'm not a big pumpkin fan, but these are good," Titus said before he picked up a macaron and tossed it in his mouth, eating it whole. The compliments made Prunella smile even more. Maude lined up her cue when she noticed Otis working on his latest drawing, piquing her curiosity. She knew Otis liked to draw and watched him do it constantly, but Maude never bothered to ask him about it. Her conversation with Gwen made her wonder just how good he was.

Her curiosity got the best of her as Maude missed her shot. Titus breathed a sigh of relief that he might have a chance to win. "That's not like you, Maude. Are you okay?" he inquired.

"Yeah, I just got distracted, that's all. You better make your shots because it won't happen again," Maude stepped away from the pool table and walked over to Otis. He wrapped his arm around his drawing so no one would see it as he leaned down to work. "Whatcha working on, Otis?"

Maude's question disrupted the ogre's concentration as he meekly looked up from his art. "Just something for art class," he said meekly. "It's a project due this week."

"Can I see it?" Maude asked, gently prodding him. Maude remembered Gwen telling her Otis hated showing his art to anyone except the teacher, but he reluctantly sat up and pulled back his arm so Maude could see his work. It was an anime-style sketch of a sword-wielding samurai riding a dragon through a futuristic cityscape. It was a perfect blending of historical fantasy with cyberpunk esthetics.

"Man, Otis, that's amazing. You've got a great talent there," Maude complimented.

"Aw, it's not that good. I've got a long way to go to be as good as Hiromu Arakawa. His art is genius."

"Yeah, but you've got a good eye, Otis. Keep at it, and you'll do just fine." Maude knew that Otis rarely received praise for his art. He smiled and nodded his head, appreciating Maude's words of confidence as he continued working on his drawing.

"Good, you're all here," Morgan said as the door opened. She strolled in, wearing a simple white mini-dress under a bolero fur coat, carrying a replica wooden puzzle box. She sauntered over to the counter and set the box down next to the tray of macarons. Morgan glared at the confection with disdain. "What are those?"

"They're pumpkin macarons with cream cheese frosting. I made them myself," Prunella said proudly. "Would you like to try one, Morgan?"

"God, no. The last thing I need is a zit breaking out on my face from all that sugar right before the Halloween dance," she complained, pushing the tray of macarons away. Maude could see how devastated Prunella was, but Morgan quickly responded to soothe her hurt feelings a bit. "I'm sure they're delicious, Prunella dear, but I can't indulge in them now. Another time, perhaps."

A smile washed across the Lamia's face, and she appeared grateful that Morgan appreciated her efforts. "Now, on to bigger and better things. I finally have everything in place to take the Pendragon. Maude, I want you and Cecilia to swap out my father's wonderful replication with the actual box tonight. Little Gwen is spending time with Triss Paul getting ready for the dance, and the lighthouse keeper has his weekly dinner with Old Lady Viv. It should be clear for you to make the exchange."

"Sounds good, so when are you going to confront Iver?" Cecilia questioned.

"At the Halloween dance. I'll give the little princess my ultimatum while the rest of you make sure no one interferes with my plan. By the end of All Hallows Eve, the Pendragon will be mine."

"What if the Spriggans interfere as they did in the cemetery?" Prunella asked.

"The Spriggans are not allowed on school grounds," Morgan explained. "Principal Cornelius knew there would be teenage angst and conflict between humans and Fae and didn't want them interfering in their education or activities, so the council granted his request. The Spriggans can only enter the school with his permission."

"So how will you convince her to give you the Pendragon, Morgan? Threaten her friends again?" Prunella asked.

"No, Prunella, dear. Nothing so blatant, but don't worry about it. I've got that part taken care of. The little princess will have no choice but to surrender her power to me."

"And then what?" Maude interrupted, causing everyone to glare at her, especially Morgan. "What are you going to do after you get the Pendragon?"

"And what do you mean by that, Maude?" Morgan asked, her voice wavering with contempt.

"I'm only asking, Morgan. What are you going to do once you get the Pendragon? I mean, the power is designed to protect the integrity of Camelot Cove and preserve the balance between Fae and humans. I can't imagine you taking on that responsibility."

Morgan appeared irritated at Maude, suddenly questioning her so openly. "Where is this coming from, Maude? Did little Gwen put you up to this?"

"Nobody put me up to anything, especially not Gwen Iver," Maude asserted. "She told me some things I need to verify myself."

"Really? Like what?"

"She said you were an ancient sorceress capable of reincarnation, the one called Morgana le Fay," Maude began. "You've been after the Pendragon for centuries, culling through the bearers since the founding of Camelot Cove, including her parents."

That admission sent shockwaves through everyone in the room. The gang thought Morgan was ambitious, looking out for herself in obtaining the power of the Pendragon, but not a murderer. She stood there and smirked at the allegations being lobbed at her. Maude took her silence as an admission of guilt.

"Nothing to say, Morgan?" Maude asserted as she continued to challenge her leader.

"What's there to say? The proverbial cat is out of the bag," Morgan said as she casually walked over to the refrigerator to retrieve a bottle of water, taking a sip before she continued. "It's true, all of it. I have tried to get my hands on the Pendragon for thousands of years. At every turn, I have been thwarted by the descendants of my accursed half-brother and his whore queen, as well as Merlin and the Lady of the Lake. Well, no more!"

She threw the water bottle at the wall, spilling it everywhere as the others braced themselves for her pending tantrum. "Once I possess the power of the Pendragon, I will be more powerful than any of them. I will reshape the world in my image and finally rid myself of this pathetic, backwater town!"

Morgan's rant shocked everyone, especially her careless disregard for Camelot Cove, the only home they had ever known. On the other hand, Maude knew how thoughtless she was toward all of them. She did not mind running scams and rackets within the community. It was a means to an end, but Maude would never think of destroying her home.

"It's true, then. You would destroy anyone or anything that got in your way of obtaining the Pendragon, including our hometown? My mother? Even me? Would you have killed me if I was the bearer?" Maude demanded an answer, but Morgan said nothing. She stared at her in silence before turning away in disgust.

"Don't you turn your back on me!" Maude screamed as she grabbed Morgan by the shoulder. Suddenly, Morgan whipped around and grabbed Maude by the throat, tightening her grip as she lifted her into the air with unimaginable strength. When Otis jumped up to help Maude, Morgan waved her other hand and fired lightning from her fingertips at the behemoth. He fell backward and crashed through the table, collapsing on the floor. Prunella rushed over to check on him while Cecilia clung tightly to Titus for protection.

"How dare you question me, you pathetic little worm! I will do whatever it takes to possess the power of the Pendragon, and if that means tearing you apart, then so be it." Maude could not reply to her as she gasped for air. "Listen to me, all of you," Morgan asserted as she leered at them. "You are here to serve me, to do as I say and nothing more. If you help me, you will be spared my wrath. Otherwise, you can join the rest of the plebians in this pathetic community and die." She tightened her grip on Maude and pulled her in close. "The choice is yours, but I would make up your mind quickly. I am not a patient woman."

Maude struggled against her but was unable to fight back. She muttered softly as she tried to catch her breath. "Yes, I will help you." Morgan smiled at the ease of her coercion before she turned to the others.

"Yeah, Morgan. We're with you," Titus said as Cecilia nodded repeatedly.

"I'll do whatever you want," Prunella fearfully added. Otis could only grumble his agreement. Morgan then released Maude and tossed her casually to the ground.

"Make sure you bring the box to me tonight," Morgan ordered as she placed her spiked heel on Maude's thigh, pressing hard into her flesh. The pain was intense as Maude glanced up at her. "And no more conversations with Gwen Iver. I don't want the little princess getting wind of my plans. Do you understand?" She pressed her heel harder and deeper into the top of Maude's leg. The pain was excruciating. She quickly nodded her head in compliance.

Morgan lifted her heel and walked away, leaving without saying another word to the gang as she slammed the door behind her. Dazed and bruised, they sat silently, wary of the powerful sorceress who left them with little choice—it was them or their home.

This year's Halloween Dance theme was "storybook characters," so getting the right outfit was essential to everyone attending. Triss knew where she and Gwen could find the right clothes. Miss Mimi's Vintage Clothing Store was filled with items dating back over a hundred years. People sold or donated their clothes to Mimi whenever a new fad or style emerged. The store was filled with everything from hoop skirts to poodle skirts, hot pants to parachute pants, shoes, hats, and vintage ties. A menagerie of clothing was hung on racks and folded neatly on tables scattered upstairs and downstairs.

Miss Mimi herself was an unusual character. She was a Gorgon, complete with snakes for hair and a gaze that could turn you to stone, but Mimi was not like her mythological figure of legend. She was a child of the 1960s and still lived there, if only in her mind. Giant sunglasses protected customers from her petrifying gaze, and her outfit of choice was a tie-dyed t-shirt and bell-bottom pants. A beautiful silk bandana kept her snake hair neatly tied up.

Triss and Gwen rummaged through the clothes racks, looking for the perfect outfit. Triss already had her costume for the Halloween dance, so she was helping Gwen find hers. However, she cringed at the storybook character her friend attempted to dress up as.

"Why on Earth did you have to pick Dorothy Gale?" Triss wondered as she scoured the racks of dresses. "I mean, talk about an old-fashioned Midwest look. That's not you, Gwen."

"She's my favorite storybook character, Triss. I've read every single *Oz* book. Besides, I didn't want to dress flamboyantly and stand out. This is my first big event as the Pendragon, so the last thing I want is to draw attention to myself."

"I gotcha, girl. I hoped for something more like a Katniss Everdeen or Alina Starkov—strong and powerful, not a timid midwestern farm girl."

"Hey, Dorothy Gale is no ordinary girl," Gwen countered. "She stood up to witches, wizards, a gnome king, and more at the tender age of twelve. That's pretty tough if you ask me."

Triss refused to argue with her as Gwen related to Dorothy so well because they were very much alike—a young girl placed in a dire situation to do whatever was necessary to save their friends from evil. Gwen was a lot stronger than she appeared to be.

"So, who are you dressing up as for the dance? You never told me," Gwen curiously queried.

"The Snow Queen," Triss said, making a royal pose. "I wanted to stay true to my Scandinavian heritage." Gwen chuckled at her outrageous assertion.

"Sorry, Triss, but you don't look like you're from any part of Scandinavia," she laughed.

*"Du vet aldri hvem noen virkelig er ved å se på dem!"* Triss said in perfect Norwegian, surprising Gwen. "It's Norwegian, meaning 'you never know who someone truly is just by looking at them.'"

"Okay, when did you learn to speak Norwegian?" Gwen stammered, shocked by her close friend's linguistic capabilities.

"You know there are a lot of Scandinavians that settled in this part of Michigan," she explained. "My dad does a lot of business with the local towns, so it helps to know the language. Besides, you ought to see the look on their faces when this Afro-centric girl speaks the language. It's priceless."

"But I still don't understand how your family could be from Norway or any other Scandinavian country?"

"Well then, you need to learn your history or mythology—however you look at it. My family of elves is known as *Svartálfar*, the dark elves from *Svartalfheim*, one of the nine realms of Asgard. So, I consider myself Norwegian by descent and believe me; I am head over heels above those blonde Scandinavians—no offense, Gwen honey."

"No problem, but I never realized you knew so much about your ancestry. How detailed is it?"

"You'll find that most of the Fae can trace their lineage back thousands of years," Triss explained. "We have longer lifespans than most humans and smaller family groups within each community."

"So not a lot of mingling among the clans—for lack of a better word, sorry—within the Fae, is there?" Gwen asked.

"Not a lot, but it has become more frequent within the past 100 years," Triss explained. "Not so much within the various races of the Fae, but definitely between Fae and humans. We have many half-breeds, but for the most part, we stick to our own."

"Here it is!" a voice cried out from the upstairs loft. Mimi strolled down the steps with a dress in hand. "I knew I had something akin to a Midwest farm dress," she exclaimed, laying it across a table of folded clothes. "It's even got the blue checkerboard print you were looking for, Gwen sugar."

Gwen was amazed that Mimi could find precisely what she was looking for in her shop's clothing chaos. "That's perfect, Miss Usala. Thank you!"

"Now, now . . . None of this Miss Usala crap. It's Mimi. And I found these, too!" Mimi held up a pair of silver low-heeled shoes and handed them to Gwen. "Now, if I remember my *Oz*, the shoes in the book were silver. They only made them red for the movie to stand out. You should be dressed 'book accurate,' not movie, yes?"

"Thank you so much, Mimi. How much do I owe you for everything?" Gwen asked, excited about the prospects for her Halloween dance costume.

"Ah, think nothing of it, sweetheart. Call it a favor for the new Pendragon, in case I 'accidentally' petrify one of my more obstinate customers," Mimi offered.

"How come she gets it for free, but I always have to pay full price?" Triss complained.

"You don't pay full price, and you know it!" Mimi snapped back. "You're one of my best customers, Triss. I always give you the best value, especially when buying in bulk."

"In bulk?" Gwen asked, looking astonished at her friend.

"Hey, a girl needs options," Triss answered as they laughed. "I've got every available space in my room packed with clothes. We can't all have a mega-closet like Morgan Moor."

"Oh, don't get me started on the 'Queen Bee' and her minions," Mimi scowled. "She dares to ask me to close up my store so she can shop without others interfering. I wasn't about to lose business just for her privacy. Still, her father came by for a 'safety inspection' and shut me down, letting his little girl look around while he conducted a fake examination of my fire exits and alarms, the son of a—oh, pardon my language, girls."

Triss and Gwen could not believe the audacity of Morgan nor her father, but they expected nothing less from the privileged priss. "Then, her pint-sized shadow, Maude Reddy, stopped by just before you two arrived. She was looking for something resembling a 'titanium weave legionnaire trench coat.' I think that's what she called it. I mean, what the heck is that anyway?" Mimi flustered, but Gwen became interested in Maude's unusual request. You can only get the Legionnaire trench coat by completing the Perdition Tower quest in the *Space Legion* video game. Gwen completed that mission, but while going through her stats and researching her cousin, she noticed that Maude had not reached that level yet.

*Why would she want something she hadn't earned in the game yet? A serious gamer like her wouldn't do that.* Gwen's quandary piqued her curiosity, especially after her earlier conversation with Maude. *What happened that rattled her so severely?* She had questions that needed to be answered, and there was only one way to get them.

"Thanks for everything, Mimi. I'll make this up to you, promise!" She grabbed her stuff and headed for the door. "I need to get home, Triss. Let's go!"

Triss had an armful of clothes but didn't want to let Gwen go off alone. "Mimi, I'll return for these after I get Gwen home. Don't you dare sell them to anyone else!" Mimi casually waved, acknowledging the demand as Triss ran after her friend. Gwen knew something was wrong. Maude had been avoiding her, especially at school. There was only one way to find out without Morgan knowing.

# Chapter Eleven:

## *The Halloween Dance of Deception*

As soon as the sun set over the lake, All Hallows Eve went into full swing throughout Camelot Cove. There was no need to hide who the Fae were on this night. This was a time of celebration for them to be who they were, as the magic that hid them disappeared with the last rays of the sun. The Fae could be amongst the human world they called home for the rest of the night.

Children dressed in their Halloween best wandered the streets, along the boardwalk and down the pier, visiting homes, stores, and even boats, asking for their tricks or treats. They chased the faeries dancing through the air and watched witches, gargoyles, and other flying creatures streak through the night sky over Camelot Cove. Besides candy, they received precious shells and stones from mermaids, undines, and selkies, and tokens of luck and magic protection from leprechauns, fauns, and imps. It was a festival of candlelight, shrieks, and scares mixed in with fun and excitement for all ages. Adults and children got caught up in the celebration with colorful and creepy costumes.

While the children scattered around town, the adults gathered in the King's Arms Hotel ballroom for the annual Camelot Cove Halloween Ball. It was a very prestigious event—by invitation only—for the most powerful and influential within the community. It was the perfect opportunity to bring them closer together in such an open environment as this.

For the teenagers of Camelot Cove, the Halloween Dance was the night of all nights. The gymnasium was decorated from floor to ceiling as the DJ blared the music. It was the first big dance of the school year for the entire student body. It was also a reversal of roles in many ways, especially tonight. With the theme of storybook characters, the Fae dressed like human characters while the humans dressed like mythological ones.

To see a goblin dressed like Atticus Finch from *To Kill a Mockingbird* or an elf dressed like Elizabeth Bennet from *Pride and Prejudice* was no different from humans dressing like fantasy characters from their favorite novels. There was even a trio—a human, an elf, and a dwarf—dressed like the three friends from *Lord of the Rings*. It was a time for them to let loose and go beyond the bounds of their secretive lives just to be themselves.

Gwen walked in with Triss, looking like stellar opposites. Gwen was the perfect Dorothy Gale from *The Wonderful Wizard of Oz,* complete with a blue-checked dress and silver shoes from Mimi, a brown wig braided with pigtails, and a wicker basket with a stuffed toy dog inside. On the other hand, Triss was glowing as *The Snow Queen* from Hans Christian Anderson. She wore a flowing lace of white over a light blue silk dress that glittered like falling snow. Even her wig and make-up were ice-themed around her face, hands, up to the tips of her ears. Her entrance was striking compared to Gwen's understated appearance, and she liked it that way.

"Wow, you two look great," Artie said, walking over to greet them. He was dressed like a hobbit from the J.R.R. Tolkien novels, complete with bare feet and large ears.

"You look good too there, Frodo Baggins," Triss commented.

"Ah, wrong. I'm Samwise Gamgee, the real hero of the trilogy, hence the frying pan as my weapon of choice," Artie corrected, waving the cast iron skillet at her.

"The hero? How do you figure that?" Triss curiously asked.

"Because if it weren't for Sam, Frodo would never have reached the Mountain of Doom to destroy the one ring. He's the true hero of that story!"

Triss and Gwen both blew it off, knowing never to question Artie regarding books. He was a consummate reader who spent his free time inside the pages of his favorite novels to avoid the machinations of his stepsister and stepfather.

"Hey, guys!" Lance shouted as he ran up to his three friends, slightly flustered. As part of the student council, Lance managed the festivities while still trying to have fun at the dance. His costume was unique; he was dressed like a dashing Prince Valiant, complete with a blue tunic, red cloak, and a pageboy wig on his head. He looked the part of a Viking prince.

"You look great, Lance, but wasn't Prince Valiant a comic strip?" Gwen queried.

"Technically, yes, but Artie reminded me it was also a graphic novel, so that counts as a storybook character," Lance argued. "Besides, being head of the committee gives me a little leeway."

"I thought 'Miss Priss' Morgan Moor was in charge of the dance committee this year?" Triss said. "Where is she?"

"Well, she hasn't shown up yet, so I've been running around taking care of things," Lance complained.

"Knowing her, she'll probably show up at the end of the night to take all the credit," Artie interjected.

"Well, I've got some more work to do, but I hope you ladies will remember to save me a dance sometime tonight," Lance said with a regal bow. Gwen and Triss curtsied in character before they all laughed as Lance headed off to deal with the next emergency.

"Hey, Triss, where's G Wayne? I thought he was coming to the dance?" Artie inquired.

"Oh, he decided to take Percy around trick-or-treating tonight," Triss explained. "His parents got invited to the big ball at the King's Arms Hotel, so Percy had no one to take him around. G Wayne volunteered to help him out, the big softy."

As the three friends wandered around the gymnasium, saying hello to friends, classmates, and social climbers, Gwen closely watched the entire room. She noticed the members of the Dreadmoor Gang situating themselves inconspicuously near all the exits. They were spread out to the four corners of the gym. Prunella was by the snacks and drinks table, serving her freshly baked goods dressed up as Julia Child from *Julie and Julia*. Otis stood by the main entrance, trying to pay no mind to anyone coming in but looking rather smartly dressed like Howl from *Howl's Moving Castle*. Lastly, Titus and Cecilia hung out near the emergency exit, keeping themselves occupied in a dark corner of the gym, decked out as *Beauty and the Beast*.

Then there was Maude, dressed in her replica *Space Legion* uniform—a trench coat with a military logo on the sleeves and shoulders, knee-high steel-toed boots, and a mock plasma rifle slung across her back. She wore game-accurate laser seeker goggles on her head and a replica communications array on her forearm. She went all out for this costume.

"Okay, how does a video game character fit all this?" Artie complained when he saw Maude.

"Well, there are several novels based on the game, so she does meet the criteria for a storybook character," Gwen explained. "I always see her carrying a different *Space Legion* book."

"Wait, you mean Maude likes to read?" Artie joked, but a glare from Gwen shut him down quickly.

"There's a lot you don't know about her," Gwen argued. "Besides, the game developers work with the writers to plant clues for certain quests within the context of the novels. It's how they keep everything within the *Space Legion* mythos canon. You can't play the game seriously if you don't read the novels."

"You seem to know much more about Maude Reddy than before. How come?" Triss queried.

"Well, we are both serious gamers regarding *Space Legion*. We've even met in-game and teamed up a few times. That was before we realized who the other was," Gwen noted, shocking both of her friends.

"Aren't you afraid she'll say something to Morgan or expose some secret?" Artie asked. Gwen shook her head vigorously.

"There's an unwritten rule the legion stands by . . . What happens in *Space Legion* stays in the frontier! Everything in the game stays there, and Maude's been cool about it.

Besides, I think things are turning around between us, a mutual understanding between cousins."

"I hope you're right. I don't trust her as far as I can throw her," Triss commented.

"I don't know. I've seen you carry a ton of bags after a shopping spree. You're stronger than you think," Gwen joked, getting a laugh out of her friend. Suddenly, the music changed from a funky, upbeat song to the first slow dance of the night. Triss spied a dozen or more girls surrounding Lance to get the first dance with him.

"I'm going to help Lance out, maybe take one of those fawning beauties for a spin," Triss hinted as she strolled toward her embattled friend. Gwen and Artie stood and watched as the floor slowly filled with humans and Fae coming together for the first slow dance. Artie squirmed in his prosthetic feet and gave Gwen a sideward glance.

"So, would you like to dance?" he finally asked. Gwen smiled, impressed that he finally got his nerve up.

"I'm not a very good dancer," Gwen remarked.

"Neither am I," Artie replied, shrugging his shoulders as he held his hand out to Gwen. "So, what have we got to lose."

Gwen took his hand, and the two walked to the dance floor, finding a good spot in the middle of the crowd. Artie gingerly placed his hands on her waist, and Gwen reached around his neck. They started to twirl to the music, taking little steps to avoid stepping on their partner's toes. It was an awkward moment for both of them, as they kept their feelings for each other to themselves.

"See, you're not so bad, even with those giant fake feet," Gwen joked.

"Yeah, well, you're not so bad yourself," Artie complimented. "I must admit, this would be easier if I weren't dancing with you."

"Me? Why me?"

"Come on; you know why," Artie stammered. "Are you going to make me say it?"

Gwen tightened her grip around his neck, pulling Artie in a little bit closer. "Uh-huh!" She smiled slyly, enjoying every moment of his uneasiness. Beads of sweat began to roll across his forehead. Gwen smirked as she waited patiently for Artie to say something. Otherwise, she may never forgive him if he decided to brush her off with no response.

"You know how much I like you, Gwen, more than just a friend," he began. "You've been there for me my whole life. I know I'm not a top scholar or athlete like Lance, but I want a chance to—" Gwen hushed him by holding her finger to his mouth.

"I think you said enough for tonight," she said. "We've got plenty of time to see where this goes, okay? Let's enjoy the dance." Gwen leaned her head against his chest as they danced to the music. The two got lost in the moment, oblivious to everyone and everything around them, until . . .

*Gwen!* A voice rang out, calling to Gwen, not in her ears but in her mind. *Gwen!* It called to her again, but an underlying evil flowed through it, giving her the chills. As the song ended, she looked around the gymnasium, looking for where the voice came from. Gwen saw Artie's confusion as his glazed eyes stared back at her.

"Are you okay, Gwen?" he asked as she continued to look around the room. Gwen became flustered but did not want to worry Artie or anyone else.

"Yeah, sorry. Excuse me, Artie, but I need to use the bathroom. I'll be right back." Gwen excused herself as she abruptly turned and walked away. She did not want Artie to worry that something he said or did set her off, but she had faith in her friend. Gwen knew it would not take him long to figure out what was wrong.

"Morgan!" she heard him say as he rushed to find the others.

Gwen ran into the girls' locker room, which was utilized as the restroom for this evening. She dropped her basket on one of the benches while looking around to ensure no one was watching her. *Gwen!* She heard the voice again, but the more it touched her mind, the angrier she grew. It felt like the voice was taunting her, which could only mean one thing.

Gwen knew who was behind it and realized this would be a fight. As much as she appreciated her friends wanting to be there to protect her, she needed them in the gym with the other students. If anything happened, the students there would need their assistance.

Gwen snuck out of the locker room and into the hallways. The lights were dim, so she walked carefully, following the voice as it led her through the empty school. The voice led her to the auditorium. Gwen opened the doors, but the theater was dark and the seats empty, with only a few spotlights lighting the stage.

She stepped cautiously, looking around the entire theater for any sign of the mysterious voice, but no one was around. "Okay, you can quit hiding. I'm here, Morgan! Show yourself!" Gwen shouted. There was silence, but then a cackling laugh grew louder. The stage lights exploded, almost blinding as Gwen covered her eyes. When the light faded, she slowly opened her eyes and finally saw her opponent.

Morgan stood in the middle of the stage, dressed as she once looked more than a thousand years ago. She wore a flowing dress of purple and gold—the colors of her royal heritage. She carried a wooden staff topped with a gold and jeweled crown. Her hands were adorned with rings of different sizes and various precious gems as valuable as the necklace, earrings, and tiara she wore. She always liked to dress above her station, but this was well above that and more.

Gwen slowly made her way down the aisle to the front of the stage, never taking her eyes off Morgan. She protected herself by summoning the armor, which looked quite out of place with her pigtails and blue-checked dress. Morgan giggled at the Pendragon in all her commoner glory.

"So, do I call you Morgan or Morgana le Fay? It's hard to tell when you're dressed like that," Gwen mocked.

"Morgana le Fay died thousands of years ago, Gwen darling. I may hold her consciousness and memories, but I'm still Morgan Moor."

"Yet it's those memories that you're acting on, chasing after the Pendragon. What are you looking for, Morgan? World domination or personal power and wealth?" Gwen's questions raised her rival's ire, but answering them would only delay the inevitable.

"It's quite simple, Gwen. The Pendragon is the primary source of magic in our world, and by controlling it, I will control anything and everything touched by magic," Morgan explained. "The Fae, spellcasters like Merlin and the Lady of the Lake, and any others like them will bow down to me to access the magic of the Pendragon. In return, I will control everything and rule over all the Fae. Nothing nor no one will stand in my way."

"Like my mother? Like all my descendants?" Gwen shot back as the anger swelled from the pit of her stomach. "I just want to hear it directly from you, Morgan. Did you kill my parents?"

Morgan laughed at her as if the question was ridiculous in its entirety. "Why on earth would you ask me a question you already know the answer to?"

"Because, for once, I want you to admit the truth. Did you kill my parents?" Gwen asked again, demanding an answer. Morgan scowled at her flippant attitude, gritting her teeth while tapping her fingernails incessantly on her staff.

"Yes, I did," she finally admitted, "and I'll do the same to everyone here unless you give me the Pendragon." Morgan sidestepped, revealing the puzzle box sitting on a stool behind her. "Maude was good enough to recover this for me, replacing it with a wonderful replica. I'm sure you or that idiot Merle never noticed the switch. Now, listen to me carefully, you insignificant little pest. You will return the power to the container so I can claim it as mine. You will do this here and now, or everyone in the gymnasium will die an agonizing and painful death."

Gwen laughed at her unbelievable assertion about life and death. "Even your little Dreadmoor Gang isn't stupid enough to take on everyone in the gym—the students, the teachers, or the chaperones."

"Oh, they're not the ones that will be doing the killing— they are!" Morgan stepped back before tapping her staff on the floor and using it to draw a circle in the air in front of

Gwen. A magic window appeared, smoke-filled and dark, until an image emerged from within.

The school was surrounded by a horde of the undead—zombies, skeletons, ghouls, and ghosts. They wandered around the building as if waiting for the order from their mistress.

"On All Hallows Eve, the bonds between the real world and the underworld are razor thin; easy for a sorceress to summon an undead army to do her bidding," Morgan said as she picked up the puzzle box and opened the lid. "Unless you relinquish the Pendragon back into the box, I will unleash all of Hell on everyone in the gymnasium. There will be some survivors, but most of them will die, particularly the humans, including dear Lance, sweet innocent Artie, and all the rest of the rabble you call friends."

"Your gang is in there, Morgan. They'll die, too!" Gwen interjected, but it only caused Morgan to laugh.

"Idiots like them are a dime a dozen, and more just like them will follow me once I possess the power of the Pendragon. Now, you have a choice—die here with your friends, or you can all live to see another day? Which will it be?" She held open the box and shoved it toward Gwen.

Gwen let out an audible sigh as it seemed the sorceress was giving her no choice. She took her armored hand and reached into the box until her arm was inside up to her elbow, but then she stopped and looked up at Morgan with a wicked smile.

"How about option three . . . I kick your ass!" Gwen swung her arm, shattering the puzzle box into pieces; it exploded with a flash of fiery brilliance. In her hand, Gwen now held a golden sword hilt with a blade of glowing light erupting from within. It wasn't a complete sword, more like a dagger, manageable for someone Gwen's size.

As the pieces of the box flew across the stage, Morgan managed to snag one piece in her hand. But the container that held the power of the Pendragon was gone. Morgan watched as Gwen filled with magical energy as she became fully integrated with the Pendragon.

"What did you do?" Morgan screamed, staring at the piece of the puzzle box in her hand.

"I did exactly what the Pendragon told me to do," Gwen responded, her blade pointed at Morgan. "This is *Caliburn*, the magic breaker. It has the power to cut through any magic, including its own. I used it to destroy the puzzle box. Now you have no way to steal the power for yourself."

"Why? Why would the Pendragon destroy its container?"

"It wasn't a container; it was a prison. That box was how people controlled the Pendragon all these years, but it finally saw a chance for freedom in me—call us mutual free spirits— and it wasn't about letting the likes of you control it. It wasn't Merle or Viv that thwarted your constant attempts to obtain the magic. It was the Pendragon itself."

Gwen smirked when she realized that her revelation startled the ancient sorceress. Morgan's mouth dropped open in panic as she stuttered breathlessly. Her eyes rattled back and forth as if desperately trying to recall her memories of past lives. "No, that's not possible. The Pendragon has no consciousness. Its form is metaphysical, nothing more."

"Wow, for someone so smart, you can be really stupid sometimes," Gwen insulted, raising the ire of Morgan. "The Pendragon is alive, like the magic that swells within it. It chooses its bearer, so of course, it has a consciousness, and for all these years, it has kept you from obtaining power. You are unworthy."

Morgan furrowed her brow, tightened her eyes, and clenched her teeth as she paced, stalking the teenager like prey. Gwen could tell she never considered the Pendragon itself fighting against her efforts to acquire the ancient magic. "You have no idea what true power is," Morgan revealed. "There is a darker power behind the Fae, and the Pendragon is unwillingly protecting it. If I don't take control, the entire human race is in danger."

Gwen remembered what Father Klaus told her about the church's warning about Armageddon starting in Camelot Cove. *Is that what he meant? Could there be a dark power behind the Fae?*

Gwen pushed her questions aside as Morgan continued to rant. "What I don't understand is how. How did you figure out my plan?" Morgan mused, growing angry at Gwen's wicked smirk.

"Because I told her!" came a shrill from the top of the auditorium. Maude strolled down the aisle, never taking her eyes off Morgan. Seeing that look of disgust and surprise was satisfying for both Gwen and Maude. "I told Gwen about your scheme to steal the box and force her to give up the Pendragon. We devised a plan to stop you, once and for all."

"You? You betrayed me after everything I did for you!"

"I never signed up for you to destroy my home, Morgan," Maude shouted. "Gwen and I don't see eye to eye on many things, but we agree on one thing. Camelot Cove is our home—the only one I've got. I wasn't about to let you destroy it."

"But I've been watching you, and my father's been keeping an eye on you too. You never met or talked over the past few days. How did you do it?"

Gwen smirked, as did Maude, at how they pulled one over on the great Morgan Moor. "Not much of a gamer, are you, Morgan?" Gwen interjected. "Maude and I met on the

Solstice Fields near Perdition Tower in *Space Legion*. She told me everything you were planning online and offered to help stop you, and she's not the only one. Your whole Dreadmoor Gang helped, too."

"What?" Morgan's one eye twitched uncontrollably, incensed as the betrayals piled on her.

"None of us wanted to lose our home to your wicked plans," Maude explained. "They're not in the gym preventing people from leaving as you wanted. They're there to stop your monsters from getting in."

"Merle and Viv didn't like the idea of me destroying the puzzle box, but the Pendragon was fine with it," Gwen added. "From now on, the bearer will be the container, and we will pass on the power to those deemed worthy, not by solving a puzzle but by the strength of their heart."

"None of that matters!" Morgan interrupted. "I will unleash the hordes of Hell on this school! Nothing can stop them, and your friends will all die!"

"Oh, don't worry about your undead army. The Spriggans are taking care of them as we speak," Gwen asserted, causing a confused Morgan to summon her viewing pane again. This time, the view was quite different. The Spriggans attacked her undead horde, clearing them from the school grounds.

"But that's not possible. The Spriggans are forbidden from entering the school!"

"I got permission from Principal Cornelius to let them on school property," Gwen said, smirking. "Once he found out about your plans, he gladly welcomed their help."

Rage swelled inside the sorceress as she turned her attention to her former protégé. "Do you have any idea what you cost me?" she screamed before she unleashed a brutal barrage of lightning arching toward Maude. Gwen leaped off the stage and landed between Maude and Morgan. Shifting from the dagger to the shield, she blocked the lightning bolt from hitting Maude.

"Don't you dare!" Gwen countered. "I won't let you hurt my cousin ever again!"

"You think your pathetic little shield can stop me?" Morgan shouted as she increased the intensity of her lightning strike. "You might possess the power of the Pendragon, but I am an immortal sorceress. An immature brat like you will not thwart my plans!"

The lightning started to push her back as Gwen tried to hold her own against Morgan's assault. A trickle of fear and doubt crept inside her for the first time. She was unsure if she could hold her own against Morgan's power until she felt a comforting hand on her shoulder. Gwen turned to see Maude standing with her.

"You're not alone, Gwen. I'm here with you." Maude winked, giving Gwen the added strength she needed. After all those years of hatred and animosity, finding some common ground didn't take long. Morgan, on the other hand, mocked their newfound camaraderie.

"You're pathetic, both of you!" she lauded. "You're nothing, Gwen Iver, but a lost little princess!"

Gwen pressed down, getting her footing in her silver slippers as best as possible. "I'm not lost, Morgan, and I sure as Hell ain't no princess." To this point, everything Gwen did with the power of the Pendragon was done instinctively, but no more. She was now in complete control. She was finally one with the ancient magic and knew exactly what to do.

Gwen swung her shield upward, sending the lightning bolt into the stage lights. The various spotlights exploded in a shower of sparks that cascaded down on Morgan, temporarily stunning her. Gwen seized her chance to strike back. She transformed her shield into a dagger as she leaped on the stage with incredible strength and agility—another newfound power emerging from the Pendragon.

Gwen aimed with precision, thrusting the blade of divine light into Morgan's forehead. The knife cut deep, not into her physical form but into the magic within her. It sliced into the web of magical connections and cut them away. The sorceress's eyes rolled back in her head, and she lost control of her body.

Gwen pulled back as Morgan collapsed on the ground, continuing to twitch incessantly. Maude made her way up on stage and stood next to Gwen. Both girls stared at the strange sight of Morgan Moor convulsing on the floor. "Is she dead?" Maude asked curiously.

"No, my blade didn't kill her. The Pendragon showed me how to use *Caliburn* to sever her magical powers, including her reincarnation ability. This is the end of the line for Morgana le Fay. Morgan Moor will be her last life in this world."

"Yeah, but why is she shaking and drooling like that?" Maude stuck her tongue out, revolted at the sight of Morgan. A mass of quivering flesh had replaced the normally prim and proper young lady.

"Separating the magic affected her mind," Gwen said as she dismissed her blade and armor. "She won't be herself for quite some time."

"Sheriff Moor isn't going to like that," Maude remarked. "He's going to go ballistic."

"I don't think even he has the power to overrule the Spriggans on this. Besides, I bet we could go into his woodworking shop and find proof that he made the replacement box. He'll have no choice but to comply or be implicated in Morgan's schemes."

They both stared uncomfortably at a helpless Morgan before Gwen finally broke the silence. "Thanks, Maude, for all your help. I couldn't have done this without you."

"I told you before, Iver, I didn't do this for you. I didn't want to lose my home or my friends."

"I know, and we still have a lot of issues between us that we need to get past. Let's call this a first step in the right direction." Gwen extended her hand in friendship. Maude paused before she finally took her hand.

"Just don't expect us to start hanging out together or having sleepovers, got it?" Maude wagged a finger at Gwen.

"How about you help me beat the Titanfall Fortress quest? I keep dying before I reach the fifth floor." Gwen and Maude discussed gaming strategy as the two walked off stage to inform the principal that Morgan had been subdued. It was the only thing these two cousins had in common, but it was a start in forming a relationship.

# Epilogue:

## *The Camelot Cove Ancestral Legacy Club*

More than a month had passed since the "Halloween Fright Night," as the Camelot Cove High School students called it. Most of them watched the battle safely from inside the gym as the Spriggans took down the undead horde wandering the school grounds. After that, most were no longer interested in dancing or hanging out together. They were more interested in watching Morgan Moor taken from the school on a stretcher, looking like a hot mess.

There was wild speculation about what happened, especially when they saw the Pendragon with Maude Reddy. Some thought that Maude turned on Morgan to gain favor with Gwen, while others questioned if the rumors about them being cousins were true. There was talk about Morgan being the reincarnation of Morgana le Fay and her attempts to steal the Pendragon, but most refused to believe it. Many saw this night as the Pendragon entering her own and Morgan Moor paying the price.

As if on cue, Sheriff Moor arrived and did precisely what Maude said he would do. He went ballistic, blaming everything on Gwen. He wanted to arrest her on the spot for assaulting his daughter. Principal Cornelius immediately stopped that, especially when Uncle Merle showed up with the fake puzzle box. When they started questioning the sheriff about where it came from and how much he knew about Morgan's plot, he reluctantly backed off and went with his daughter to the hospital.

In the weeks that followed, Artie moved out of his home. Sheriff Moor kicked him out, upset that his stepson sided with Gwen Iver over Morgan. He wanted nothing to do with him. Fortunately, Viv stepped up and became Artie's guardian, and he moved in with her. He even changed his last name, dropping the Moor surname for his mother's maiden name, Eigr. It was a new start for Artie.

Morgan was transferred to the Northern Lakes Mental Health Facility in mainland Michigan for care while she recovered from losing her magical powers. Her father stepped down as sheriff to care for his daughter during her extended recovery. Her fractured mind continued to reform, leaving her empty and in a near vegetative state. She spent her days looking out the window, twirling the piece of the puzzle box between her fingers. Morgan would not let it go or put it down. She held it tightly as if something deep inside hoped for a spark of magic to return.

Gwen and the others decided this event called for a deeper investigation into this so-called "dark power" behind the Fae. Triss had no idea what Morgan was referring to, and neither did her father. The other clan elders of the Fae were equally in the dark as they were several generations removed from the founders of Camelot Cove. Gwen did not trust speaking to Viv and Merle about this—not yet, at least—until they knew more.

To that end, Gwen and the others decided to form an after-school club to catalog and investigate things further. Even Principal Cornelius offered to assist as an advisor, ensuring things stayed in order. They called it the Camelot Cove Ancestral Legacy Club, bringing together humans and Fae to protect their home from harm—outside or within the community.

Principal Cornelius walked into the classroom. To his dismay, his students had already started without him. Triss and Gwen were working with Lance on a comprehensive list of the Fae races, while G Wayne and Artie were using his laptop to cross-reference various strange and unanswered events in Camelot Cove over the past decades.

Cornelius liked their progress and was encouraged by their enthusiasm for the project. He was also unaware of this "darker power" behind the Fae, which troubled the educator. During his long life, he vaguely remembered rumors of an entity "pulling the strings" behind the scenes, as it were, but his clan put it off as superstitious nonsense. They were logical beings, dealing with facts, not hearsay.

However, the fact that Morgan Moor, a.k.a. Morgana le Fay, spent her many lifetimes trying to acquire the Pendragon to fight this presence legitimized the possibility of this dark power. It was worth investigating further, so these brilliant young minds were the most adaptable at this. Gwen did not want Merlin or the Lady of the Lake to know about this, but Cornelius knew better. He would keep them in the loop to ensure the safety and well-being of the Pendragon and her friends.

"Excuse me, Principal Cornelius," Maude said, surprising the educator. His head spun around, shocked to see the former Dreadmoor Gang standing in the doorway. Before he could question anything, Gwen spoke up.

"Hey, Maude, glad you all could make it!" Gwen said as she rushed over to greet them.

"I brought cookies," Prunella exclaimed, holding up a box of her latest confections.

"Finally! I'm starving!" Artie shouted as he ran over to help her set out the treats. "Ah, these are better than last time, Prune. Thanks for bringing them!"

"I'm learning so much more working for the Peter's," Prunella explained. "I'll bring donuts next time."

"You are not helping my diet, Prune honey. I have got to watch my girlish figure," Triss exclaimed before picking up a cookie, enjoying the flavor of the delicious confections. All these compliments made Prunella very happy.

"Hey, Maude, I wanted to ask you about some strange events we've already discovered. Maybe see if any of them ring a bell with you," Artie asked.

"Sure, sounds good. Titus and Cecilia might know more about them since they're always breaking curfew," Maude remarked, earning a shove from the minotaur.

"Hey, you've broken curfew a few times yourself, Maude," Titus argued, but they all laughed as the three helped Artie and G Wayne with their research.

"We're having trouble with the ogre family tree, Otis. How much do you know?" Lance asked the ogre.

"I know a few stories my grandma told me. I don't know how much it would help," Otis replied, scratching his head.

"Any little bit will help, big guy. I've always found that the best truths are buried deep within those family stories," Gwen added, bringing him over to the board to review what they already had.

These new interactions between former rivals surprised even Principal Cornelius. Gwen noticed a smile fall across the educator's face. She hoped their efforts in bringing Fae and humans together would make him proud. Gwen would ensure there was hope for the future of Camelot Cove.

Deep within the earth, faerie lights lit the way as he begrudgingly staggered down the dark path. With every hoof step clamoring off the stone walkway, the residents of *Tír na nÓg* knew better and cleared a way for the Faerie King Oberon. The faun moved briskly along the path after a short visit to the outside world. He had to confirm the reports personally. Otherwise, his beloved wife would not believe him. At times, that was all he was to her—a simple messenger relaying news of the outside world.

When he stepped into *Tír na nÓg*, you would never know you were miles underground. The air was crisp and clean without the pollution generated by human technology. Sunlight basked across forests and meadows with flowing streams and deep clear water ponds scattered about the sacred land. The trees were massive, hundreds of feet tall, and just as wide, like skyscrapers in a city skyline, as staircases wound around and across the tree line.

Oberon ignored the pleasantries of those he passed by as he made his way to the heart of *Tír na nÓg*—The Petal Dawn Throne in the Plain of Honey. It was an open field in the heart of the forest where a giant flower lay open near the base of the meadow. The tulip always bloomed and changed its color depending on the mood of the Faerie Queen Titania as she sat on the Petal Dawn Throne.

Faerie Queen Titania was the epitome of beauty and was loved by all in the fairy kingdom of *Tír na nÓg*. Her hair glistened white, like pure starlight on a midsummer night.

Her skin was covered in a frock of white lace, fair as the flower petals in a field of daisies blooming in springtime. Her wings were unlike regular faerie wings, more like that of a butterfly as rainbow-hued colors spread across them.

She watched her husband approaching breathlessly before wistfully shooing away her servants as they tended to her. "So, dear husband, what news from the outside world? Was Morgan successful in retrieving the Pendragon this time?" she asked in a voice that could melt newly fallen snow with warmth and an inviting tone.

"I'm afraid not, my love. It seems this incarnation of Morgan le Fay was as flawed as all the others," he exclaimed. "The new bearer of the Pendragon, Gwen Iver, even destroyed the container—the ancient puzzle box. She is in full possession of the power."

"All the better, dear Oberon. We take it for ourselves. I'm sure this little human is no match for the might of *Tír na nÓg*. It would be the perfect time to strike."

"I believe caution might be prudent on our part, sweet Titania," Oberon said as he moved closer to the throne. "It seems Morgan may have revealed information about us to the Pendragon. Our followers in Camelot Cove say this child, Gwen Iver, is asking questions about a 'dark power' behind the Fae."

"Dark Power? Me? Titania of the Morning Dawn? Why would someone refer to me as a 'dark power' of the Fae?"

"Personally, my darling Titania, I think it's that priest's doing, but I digress," Oberon lamented, hoping to appease his wife. "In any case, we should proceed cautiously now that dear little Morgan is powerless and locked away."

"What? The most powerful sorceress in the world? How is that possible?" Titania clamored.

"Well, it seems the new wielder of the Pendragon cut her strings, as it were, not only severing her ability to reincarnate but her access to magic too," Oberon explained. "The whole process has severely affected her mind. It will be some time before we can rely on her again."

Oberon could see Titania hanging on to his every word. He was never cautious, but his insights on this proved quite revealing. "I see what you mean, darling Oberon. This Gwen

Iver needs further investigation to determine how best to deal with her. For the sake of the Fae, we must capture the Pendragon or destroy it."

# ~ THE END ~

The adventures of the Pendragon in Camelot Cove continue in

*Gwen Iver & The Mermaid's Curse*

# About The Author

Mark Piggott, a native of Phillipsburg, New Jersey, enlisted in the U.S. Navy in 1982, beginning a 23-year career. He served on four aircraft carriers and various duty stations as a Navy Journalist before he attained the rank of Chief Petty Officer. He retired from active duty in 2006. Mark currently works as a writer-editor for the Department of Housing and Urban Development. He and his wife, Georgiene, reside in Alexandria, Virginia. They have three children.